The author walked the Camino (an ancient pilgrimage route in Spain) for the first time in 2003. 2022 was his fourteenth summer walking the Camino. He has also walked along pilgrimage trails in Palestine, Israel, Nepal and Italy. This novel, *Miri*, an allegory of the Camino experience, steps into the pain, the joys, the feeling of magic as well as the reality of the journey and the transformation(s) each pilgrim will come to face.

Miri

Yunus Sola

Miri

Vanguard Press

A CIP catalogue record for this title is
available from the British Library.

ISBN 978 1 80016 618 9

*Vanguard Press is an imprint of
Pegasus Elliot Mackenzie Publishers Ltd.*
www.pegasuspublishers.com

First Published in 2023

**Vanguard Press
Sheraton House Castle Park
Cambridge England**

Printed & Bound in Great Britain

For an angel

My gratitude to Cindy and Monica for the original spark and to all the pilgrims I have walked alongside on the Camino for their inspiration, hope and love.

1

Existence

When the seven voices sang to Miri in one euphony, 'You have been a part of me for all of the past, and now it is time to be yourself,' Miri understood the moment had arrived. A moment for her spirit to be born. For her to enter a new realm, a new world, and experience a new existence that some called 'life'.

The spirit was surprised, and she had never been surprised before. She found the song and the voices comforting. Until that moment, comfort, surprise and other notions such as anticipation had no meaning to Miri.

The word 'life' was nothing less or more than a sound, a mystery to spirits. But with the final resonance of the song, Miri became overwhelmed with an uncertainty she instantly knew was hope. The surprise of knowing did not overwhelm her. And when a warmth, very satisfying, flowed inside and around her, she wondered if this was the feeling associated with the word love. Love was more than a sound, more than a word. Love would be a unique feeling. All spirits knew love could only be experienced in the state that she was now being taken to, life.

Even if experiencing love was the only purpose of life, Miri could not help but wonder the new enigmas she would soon face. She would view the universe from a new point, from a new place, a new consciousness, through the sensations of a physical being, and be subject to an idea called time.

And even as the birthing began, even before her body had embraced the first song, the seven voices rose again to sing for Miri.

'And when you are ready, when we are in need of you, you will again return to us.'

If Miri did not know already, she immediately understood that her journey from divine spirit to the world of life would lead to her birth.

And, it would also lead to her death.

As threads of the universe began to unravel around her and she let her spirit enter the thread that would carry her, Miri consumed the consequence of the songs. Whatever was about to happen, she knew she was about to leave her spirit existence, depart from the only space she had ever known. One takes nothing from one existence to the other. She would never again remember the words of the euphony, and while remnants of a past existence sometimes remain as a faded memory within a sensation, she would never know her spirit being ever again.

But then, just as she allowed the thread of life to grip her and she gave permission to her spirit being to flow into the new realm called consciousness, before the moment could complete itself, Miri was caught by an unintended reverberation. An echo appeared to reach out to meet her.

Miri looked towards the unexpected moment, another tiny thread, an echo had crept out of the complexity that was the universe.

To the new spirit-life, still in transformation, within the yarn of the fugitive echo there appeared a face. To her new body, to Miri's half-developed inquisitive being, the face was nothing less than irresistible. Miri reacted the only way her body was designed to in such a moment of confusion, surprise and desire, her sixth sense reached out with one of her tiny hands and grasped tightly the look upon the face. It was spontaneous, unplanned, and, most probably, unintended. Miri was not supposed to do anything other than be born. Most certainly, she was not supposed to grab hold the look of an angel.

For the angel concerned, the angel to whom the face belonged, the entire moment was nothing less than a fraction of space, for angels do not have knowledge of time. To the spirit of Miri's mother, Amma, about to give birth, the consequences felt like an eternity.

Amma might have narrated an epic story, relived her entire life all over again. She might have explained her past and foretold her future. But Amma only understood the pain of labour which lasted so many hours that Amma demanded that all the clocks be removed and an eight series box set of her favourite Korean soap opera be looped on a small screen in the birthing room. Miri, having already entered the gate to her new being called life, sensed nothing other than her Amma's delight and heartbeat.

The labour was long. One of the longest in the history of all births. For, in clenching the moment from the spirit world, Miri's transformation had paused, and the pause had led the new child-being into a hesitation. The universe should have been confused. What had this new being, this perfect new life, clenched and extracted from the spirit world? What new balance, or imbalance, had she created?

But a universe is never confused. Universes have never been known to panic. A universe knows all about unknowns, for unknowns, eventually, always become knowns. And all knowns have a consequence.

The consequence to the newborn child, if she survived the birth, would be a hand that held the look of an angel. A look that saw the purpose and future of all humankind. A hand that held a consequence.

The consequence for the universe remained to be discovered.

2

Birth

While Amma and Miri were wrestling with life and the new dawn, the valley, a little valley in northern Spain, the valley where Miri was about to be born, was eerily silent. Instead of the wake-up and breakfast routines before the school runs and the weekly farmer's market, the tremors that had begun at dawn, and now followed the sun into the daylight, firmly held the valley to ransom demanding unconditional surrender. There would be no rhythm of traffic jams this morning. Quiet terror and silent panic replaced the fruit and vegetables in the plastic-free shopping bags.

But not even the possibility of more tremors could halt the daily morning meditation to the local *panadería* for the fresh bread and confirmation of hope that life was still worth waking up for. But today's bread had not been baked and so the hope faltered. Instead, villagers gathered in little whispers and little mutterings along the *calle*, in the plazas, but the most uneasy silence was in the bars where the Spanish breakfast TV arrested the eyes and ears of everyone passing.

As the morning coffee-calmed voices began to relive accounts of the tremors in the dreaming darkness of slumber, some attempted to laugh away their anxiety, many feared the next tremor, others, still in shock, were unable to feel or fear. The collection of words in the bars carried listeners into a scary horror movie, making everyone wonder what mystery had kept them alive.

'The bed began to shake. It was a nightmare. I did not know if it was real.'

'The walls were moving like the waves of the sea.'

'I dreamt I was on a boat moving fast and out of control in the rapids of the river.'

'I was half sleep. I did not understand what was happening and did not even leave my bed. I just turned over and told myself it was not real. It would stop. When it did not stop, of course it was real, my heart jumped. The ceiling could have collapsed on top of us. My family and I are lucky to be alive.'

Some of the lighter sleepers who had left their beds and their homes in the night during the tremors, even described accounts of a pink ethereal light painting the town.

'I saw pink snowflakes,' a number of witnesses convinced each other.

'The stars were breaking up and falling to earth, it was stardust.' One or two allowed their imagination to wander.

'Do not colour the tremors with your dreams.' A few suffering voices attempted to make sense with their wisdom while keeping their eyes firmly on the constantly updating TV news ticker tape. 'Only the tremors are real.'

Few had noticed the silence of the smart phones. Only when the phone handset signals suddenly burst alive with beeping messages and ringing as tearful relatives checked on their loved ones did the reality of the moment, the danger and potential loss of love, dawn on the villagers. No loss of life or injuries had yet been reported in the valley. Some of the houses in the town exposed their weaknesses and their cracked skins were hastily being checked by a team of town engineers and emergency services. A few homes were being evacuated and their doors sealed. As a precaution, all roads within the tremor zone were closed. Schools in the valley would remain shut today. Night shifts across the valley would not return home until all the roads and bridges had been checked and the engineers posted the all clear. Many began to wonder if the pink glow in the night had been a dream after all.

Sensing the urgency, and while volunteers gathered outside the Estación de Bomberos to help survey the town, the roads and to reclaim the valley, for those on the night shift in the maternity unit where Miri made ready to enter a hospital room, a room dressed in white; there had been no pause.

Under the shade of a protected six-hundred-year-old heavily burdened oak tree, was a room in a birthing clinic in northern Spain where Amma was nearing the end of her strength and her patience.

Her husband could not bear to look at the pain and

the life draining from Amma's frail, tired and weak body.

'Save her,' he begged the nurses and the doctors.

The lead doctor guided the husband out of the door.

'Whatever we do, one will die,' she explained, quietly.

Appa wept. 'Save her.' And he wept even more.

In the clean delivery room, a wet and sticky Miri was finally welcomed by the warm arms of a delighted and grateful but very weak new mother. Grateful that the labour was over. But the tiny pink feet also held an almost blue face, and before Amma could fully embrace the empty life in her hands, and before she could miss her family, who were many thousands of kilometres away in South Korea, a flurry of activity and foreign words filled the room.

Since Amma had lived, to the wet-faced relief of her husband, nurses and doctors, Miri was not expected to do so. But this happened to be the most advanced maternal hospital in northern Spain hosting the most experienced surgeons in the medical world for complicated births.

Unable to drive home to a waiting family who had already prepared a retirement breakfast party, a surgeon sat patiently in the hospital staff restroom. A room that also held the best views of a valley but today held a window containing a misty white morning and an embarrassed dawn. Today's sunrise was supposed to bring new light to mark the end of his long professional career in the theatre room. The dawn was supposed to welcome him to a well-used armchair of unread newspapers, endless café con leche and pre-recorded TV dramas and documentaries, not to mention long walks and mountain treks he had planned with his wife. Instead, he sipped a coin-slot prepared cup of hot, milky, Cola Cao while seated on an indifferent hospital staffroom chair. He wondered if the chair also held the beginning of the end of his life.

A silent newborn is not extraordinary. Many are born soundless. It is well-known that newborns occasionally need a little encouragement and some reminding. Reminding that the warmth of mother's life-giving birth fluid and the comfort of her constant heartbeat was in the past, that the newborn was in a new world, a new future with new sounds and a new warmth of a sun that offered endless hope.

But, unlike other newborns, this newborn bore the shocking silence, burdens and cold of the embarrassed, limp oak tree which had forgotten the warmth of the sun. And when little Miri was being reminded to leave her nine-month-old memory behind, and step into her new world, the doctors were surprised when her body trembled. Had hope found its way into Miri's tiny little body? As the combined effort around her continued, her little body shuddered again, her muscles both reacting and fighting against all expectations of silence and death.

'She is alive!' screamed a surprised nurse, smiling

at the struggle and the battle and the hope in front of him.

'She is having a seizure; call the specialists, the surgeons. She may yet live to feel her mother's love,' called the doctor.

Miri's exit from the birth room was rapid. Amma and Appa prepared for both grief and joy. For none could say which would be the outcome.

Little Miri did not like to be reminded that she was somewhere new, did not like the feel of the present or the future.

3

Life

Amma was inconsolable. She had fed the life inside her, felt life grow inside her, move inside her, she cherished meeting her newborn, but this was not the union she had imagined. There had been no sign, no messages in the stars, in the planetary alignment with the moon, in the sounds of the newly hatched cabbage-white butterflies that had overwhelmed Amma's house during her pregnancy, or in the scents of the pink and white orchids that had flowered continuously on the verges around Amma's house for the past 271 days. Nothing had whispered that the child would not wish to meet her mother on the day of the birth in this snow-white hospital room. And Amma, being so far from her family home, a family ten thousand kilometres away on the other side of the world, wondered if she had made the right decision to move across countries and oceans to be with the one she loved. Her husband had nurtured a lifelong ambition to create the best wines, to work in the famous wine region of Rioja in a strange and wonderful land where the cooked rice in Valencia was called paella and the beautiful music in Andalucía was called Flamenco.

Had Amma been in South Korea she would have been surrounded by a comforting family who would have explained what was happening, why everything was happening. Her parents would have lit incense sticks and called on the gods. Priests and family members would have been dispatched to the temples to pray for Miri.

Amma had never felt so alone, so vulnerable. She did not need to understand the language being spoken around her, or an explanation or a translation of the silent tears of her husband to know that Miri, her first born, might live a little longer, but may soon die.

And so she reached out the only way she knew how, she prayed. She prayed to her God — who also happened to be everyone else's God — that the child be given a strong heart, a loving heart, a heart that would beat to the pulse of the life of that tiny, perfect little body, be given the first taste of Spanish air in her lungs, be given a desire to live, to make her first sound, to see the birds and flowers and to hear the brilliant, rhythmic, local music. But most of all, she prayed that little Miri would have a wish to meet her mother.

A newborn laying on an operating table is perplexing. Very difficult for everyone — even if around the operating table are the world's most noted surgeons and published experts. Tiny veins for the anesthetist's needle to find, tiny cuts to make, tiny hearts to repair, no room for error. But the surgeon, who should have retired and been on his way home to his waiting armchair, had even more hope than all those in the operating room. He could not allow his last charge to meet death. He would not carry to his armchair, as his last act, the image of a limp, dead child on his operating table, or the memory of the faces of grief on a newborn's mother and father.

The surgery was long. The hours following Miri's surgery felt longer still. The day's endless news about the earthquake continued on all the local and national TV channels. Those in the hospital who could, listened to the reports of the first recorded earthquake in the region. And those on duty in the maternity ward, including the surgeon, commenced what they hoped would be their final hospital round of their extended shift. The surgeon was unsuccessful at hiding his fear as he approached little Miri's mother and Amma noticed his wince.

Catching Amma's eyes, the surgeon confessed his shock and surprise at what he had found on the operating table. This being his last-ever shift, his last-ever case, his last surgery, the daylight being the beginning of his retirement, what he had seen on the operating table made him wonder if it had been a portent, an augury of his life's work.

Was his life being measured?

Was the remainder of his future being written?

Was his afterlife being written and prepared?

Being a professional, the surgeon put his superstitions and fears aside for a moment. The surgeon paused. He met both Miri's Amma and Appa's eyes and explained why the baby had been silent, had entered a seizure; describing something he had never seen before, hoped never to see again. Little Miri, he said, was born with four hearts and, when woken, each heart was frantically beating to its own rhythm. With each beat of each frenzied heart, her tiny, perfect, and frail little body was sinking into itself and descending into chaos and bedlam.

'My team and I have done what we can. Now we wait,' he said. 'And if the baby survives, and I remain alive and have the strength to do so, I have made a prayer to my God to fulfil a promise to carry today's blessings to a saint who is waiting in an ancient cathedral along a road that leads to the end of the world.'

Amma did not understand the words but heard the words and already knew their meaning, even before Father's translation confirmed her fears. She cried, she sobbed; was her God so cruel to want to take her first child? What would her God do with the life of a newborn? What need did her God have with the perfect little body? And so she prayed even more. She even wondered if the Saint waiting in the ancient cathedral along the road that leads to the end of the world was listening and would understand Korean.

The universe is always listening. Ever since the universe was created and living beings found themselves dancing to the beats of their hearts, hearts have learnt to listen and drum to the very many reverberations around them. When each little heart inside Miri heard the beats of the other hearts, they began to listen to one another, sing with one another, play jazz and settle into a very particular beat, a special rhythm, an exceptional tune, a music that would forever echo through her body and fill the silence of the universe.

As 'Safe' and 'All Clear' signs began to be posted, relief gently began to replace the silence on the roads and bridges that had been closed since the morning. Although piecemeal and late, the day's hospital shift began to arrive to the delight of the night staff.

The surgeon, with some anxiety, had only just begun his debrief and the handing over his notes for his final case, when an excited nurse interrupted and asked the surgeon to check on Miri. Reaching the recovery room, the surgeon was shocked to see the newborn breathing freely and waking. Removing the child from the incubator and listening to her hearts, the surgeon swore he felt a rhythm, he convinced himself he was hearing music. But he had to put the thought behind him, for he was a professional.

He insisted upon carrying Miri to her mother. As he walked past a silent family in the ward, silent parents with their sleeping and silent newborn, and laid Miri upon Amma's waiting arms, the surgeon prayed and gave thanks for the gift of his skill, for the span of his career, for forgiveness for his past errors. He was moved by this final case, the last child he would treat. He gave thanks for the child's fortune, kissed the tiny child's eyes and whispered so only her mother would hear,

'Only angels and devils are born with more than one heart; this child is an angel.'

4

Hari

To many, Hari was an angel. But in a universe that contains so many spirits, spirits with many forms and many purposes, Hari only knew the purpose that he had been given, Hari was a collector in a realm that many called, the living. Hari was a Collector of Burdens.

Mothers of newborns carry many burdens. They often call on the burden collector when the moment is too heavy to bear. Hari thought nothing of the relief that was offered once the burdens were collected. Spirits did not know relief.

But in this moment of collection, Hari sensed a pause in the universe. To living beings, the pause might feel like a missing heartbeat. To a spirit, who has no knowledge of time, the pause might have lasted for eternity. A new world or an entire universe might have been created in that pause. And so Hari found himself drawn into the pause.

Hari saw, inside this pause, an energy that did not belong amongst the living. The energy had no right to be in the living world. The force of energy, the consequence of the presence of the energy, held him, his gaze. And so Hari met little Miri's hand for the first time.

Hari had seen newborns before. But newborns did not carry burdens and Hari had never looked at, or paid attention to, or approached one. Yet this child drew him. This little child carried a weight far greater than all the burdens he had ever collected. Hari instantly sought guidance within the patterns of the universe. Every thread had a pattern. Every movement of every particle in the universe had a purpose, markers, guides, and right now, they were all pointing at Miri. So he continued to look. And as Hari looked deeper, he followed the threads of the universe to the mystery Miri held in the palm of her hand.

But wherever he looked, Hari found no explanations, no replies, only more mystery. The consequence of that moment had not yet been written.

Hari knew.

And Hari was not supposed to know anything.

The clenched tiny palm of the newborn held a power the child was not deemed to possess.

But when Hari tried to draw closer to the new born, he was puzzled. The newborn was out of his reach.

Spirits should not be puzzled. Spirits cannot approach newborns.

Spirits cannot see the mystery that protects newborns, they do not know the joy of a mother and father's love, or understand the divine force that creates life. Few would know that the love of creation combined with a parent's love is far more powerful than any spirit.

Hari did not know, and Hari could not approach Miri.

Hari was a spirit. Hari did not know love. Any kind of love. Let alone a mother's love. When he saw the frozen fist, when he understood he could not approach, Hari became aware of his first realisation. And spirits were not supposed to realise anything.

Hari wanted to know love.

On the Mountain of Oaths, all angels charged to serve in the realm of the living, the realm of humans, animals and all living creatures, are required to take an oath to protect and never to harm any living being.

Being ascribed the task to collect their burdens, Hari freed living beings from torment. Some beings called their burdens a torture, others called them demons. But demons were another spirit entirely. Hari knew demons. Demons was the name given to angels or spirits that had refused to take the oath on the Mountain of Oaths.

Being so close to the child, unable to touch the mystery in her frozen hand, the moment carried Hari to the Mountain of Oaths. Time had no meaning to spirits. Now and then were the same moment.

Just like demons, Hari could have rejected the oath.

'Do not take the oath,' the angel protestors called to him. 'Humans are weak, only clay. Do not take the oath, do not serve these weak fragile creatures. Are we not better than them?'

To Hari, the universe was one. There were no

divisions between one being and another. Differences had no meaning. Every being, every particle, was part of the one universe, he did not understand or accept the notion of "being better".

He took the oath.

Why had the child brought, or been allowed to bring, a little piece of the force from the other realm? He felt the imbalance. And inside that imbalance he sensed a power. A power almost as great as the universe.

How could a being, so small, so vulnerable, carry a power, and not even be aware of the potential that it held?

What would be the consequence of the moment?

Why had he taken the oath to protect these living beings?

Why was Hari even asking questions? Hari had never asked questions before.

The questions were curious.

Hari did not know love, and in that moment, knowing he could not approach the child because of the mystery of love, he became obsessed with the need to know love. He had never wanted anything before. He had never understood what it was to want. But he knew that in this newborn, within that tiny, clenched fist, was a mystery, a power that had the answer to his new questions, his desire to understand love. Why was love so important? Why was life created to feel love, to understand love, to know love, and even to reject love? Hari wanted to know.

Want! A word, a feeling that seemed to sink him, make him feel smaller, it made him feel less. And the less he felt, the more Hari knew that he had to possess the power that lay hidden in this child's clenched fist.

The force could teach the spirit about life, love and time.

With the force, he could also destroy all the love in the world, sabotage time, and destroy the very purpose of life.

What would he do with the force?

The answer was already within Hari.

'Spirits cannot know love, so why should humans?'

5

Faces

Newborn Miri felt her Amma's and Appa's love.

A love that heals.

After the trauma of the birth, with her Amma and Appa's love, Miri's hearts healed.

Miri's mother and father did not heal.

Amma and Appa's bedroom pillows and their bedroom walls held the memories of silent tears and screaming fears, but they made sure no one saw the wounds and scars that trauma leaves behind.

Little Miri only knew love. She did not know about trauma, tears or that her life would be short. And she most certainly had no knowledge that her body and her talents had any limits and barriers. And so she danced her way through the streets of her childhood. She heard the phenomenal music of her hearts. A rhythm that encased her. A music only she could hear. And everyone in the village who watched Miri dance could do nothing other than watch in awe.

Through her dance, Miri expressed a deep feeling, an emotion that she seemed to be drowning in but could not ascribe a word to, love. She loved in a way that only she could, a love that only four hearts can offer. A love quadrupled with intensity. When she saw love, she danced love. And every step of her dance expressed the love that she saw, the shine of every smile of love, the scream that accompanied every laugh that came from love. And if that was not enough, every dance contained a touch and an embrace that shone love.

Miri was easy to love.

Miracles, somehow, make themselves easy to love.

Four hearts, somehow, make it easy to know love.

As Miri grew, hospital visits, blood tests, scans and annual corrective surgeries became a normal cycle of life for Miri. Miri's parents made sure the surgeons and nurses were showered with Korean praises, embraces and kisses. Miri's Amma always wondered why the universe had brought her to Spain, to that hospital on the night of the birth. She could have been in Korea. In fact, her husband could have found employment anywhere in the world. But anywhere else and the newborn, Miri, would not have survived.

Why him? The surgeon would also wonder. What forces had kept him at the hospital, in that chair, in the staff room at the time of Miri's birth? He was supposed to have retired in the early hours of the morning before Miri's birth. Miri's survival was a miracle, all the surgeons agreed. But they also knew the clouds of uncertainty and the tears of love and pain that accompany miraculous survivals.

How long would Miri live? The surgeons asked every year after the annual scans and tests on Miri's hearts were analysed. And every year, the surgeons were surprised. Miri did not just heal after one surgery, she healed quickly after every surgery. But the surgeons made sure to temper all expectations. Surgeons are trained to speak with both caution and honesty.

'She has healed again but know that the repair is not permanent. Hearts are complicated and Miri's remain weak. We do not know how her hearts will manage and accommodate the needs of her growing body. But with rapid advances in surgery, and the miracle of her healing after every surgery, anything is possible.'

Mother and father knew what the words meant. The surgeons could not say if Miri would live to experience her teens.

'We will never give up,' said her father.

And sensing overprotective parents, 'Fresh air,' the staff at the hospital insisted. 'Keep her active. Let her play. Let her run, let her dance. Let her fall and stand again, alone. Allow her body to build strength and stamina. Her body must learn her limits.'

Encouraged, Amma and Appa planned outings. Miri danced during picnics in the park, weekend camping outings in the forests, and the uphill and downhill treks in the Pyrenees.

Miri would dance all the way to the weekly market and back home again. And the dance did not stop in the supermarket, or the local pizzería, it continued even in the Thai takeaway.

The spirit inside Miri's soul was strong, stronger

than her body. Life continued to grow inside her and her spirit continued to heal the vessel that contained her. And much to the surprise and gratitude of everyone whose life she touched, loved and embraced, the same people who had made ready for grief, the child grew and met her teen years.

Miri's rapidly growing body met more surgeries. And more teenage moods and teenage personalities than her parents would have liked to have been introduced to. Miri survived every mood change and every surgery. And when the surgeries stopped just before her rapidly growing teen years, and Miri continued to dance and walk to school, there was a sense of relief.

Miri survived. Miri's body calmed.

But while Miri managed to conquer her body, one discomfort Miri could not conquer was an itch that resided inside the palm of the frozen fist of her left hand.

There were times the itch was so severe that Miri would scream and run to the kitchen, put her hand on the chopping board and demand, in fact plead, that the hand be chopped off. To begin with, the theatre made Amma and Appa laugh hysterically, but the humour rescinded the day she was found in the kitchen, sobbing, with the large chopping knife in one hand and the offending arm on the kitchen top ready to be sacrificed.

Of course, no one chopped off her hand. Everyone tried to help Miri with different tools to relieve the monster inside the offending itch. Fortunately, there was a tiny, fleshy, gap under the thumb of the frozen fist.

And the gap, Miri discovered, led directly to the palm where the itch festered. Like any problem solving youngster, various long implements were found, adapted, and inserted into the hole and their impact on the itch affected area explored.

The trouble was, any item within reach, even long and sharp instruments were forced, pushed or squeezed into the palm. Often with very bloody outcomes.

Respite came one day in, of all places, an international chain coffee shop in Barcelona during a family shopping weekend. Her father loved his café con leche while mother loved exploring the neighborhoods. Father and daughter had tired walking through the maze of streets around the synagogue. A coffee shop was the perfect place to retreat.

'Let's try some Italian coffee,' Appa suggested.

And it was here Miri discovered the perfect itch gratifying implement. Long plastic stirring rods with rounded ends.

Miri's eyes lit up as soon as she saw one and her pockets had to be stretched to be filled. Her father begged the coffee shop manager for more and even paid for them to courier a box home. Soon, thanks to an internet shopping website, hundreds of itch-relief rods occupied every hidden corner of the home, the car and even the school mochila.

The itch problem was resolved. Miri was satisfied. She could focus her attention on other things like playing and growing up and seeing love.

Miri had always seen love.

Miri had learnt to recognise love, all forms of love. And unlike others, she saw love.

And when she was well into her teenage years, Miri began to understand why she had been told, since a very young age, never to repeat, never to discuss what she saw, to keep her gift secret from everyone. A gift that made her strange and different, both feared and loved.

Every time she came across love, love in any form, she saw the face of an angel.

6

Forest of Covens

When she was two and a half years old, Miri managed to string her first four-word sentence together. For Miri it was a momentous moment. She had suddenly realised how to communicate her vision, with her mother, with words. And she was very excited to share what she saw.

For her mother, however, who was feeding Miri and attempting to teach a left-handed Miri to hold a spoon with her right hand, the words that came from Miri's mouth were not just a surprise, but a source of great distress.

The moment began innocently enough.

'Face.' Miri pointed towards her mother's left shoulder.

Mother smiled as she guided Miri's hand that held the spoon, full of home-made seasonal fruit purée, towards Miri's mouth.

'Yes, face,' Amma humored soothingly, repeating Miri's word. 'Clever girl. Open wide, yummy.' The food and the spoon holding was the only priority in that moment. Miri had already missed her mouth a few times and her face was already a multicolored photograph that could have been sold to a baby magazine for the front cover.

'Angel,' Miri persisted, looking and pointing again towards her mother's left shoulder.

Mother had not heard Miri use that word before. A fresh new word she thought. The focus still on the coordination of holding the spoon firmly, guiding Miri's hand towards her open mouth.

Maybe Miri had heard Amma praying? Was the word on a children's television programme? Amma rattled her brain. The clinic, the hospital, the doctors and nurses? Amma imagined many explanations. Where did Miri hear the word angel?

Her Amma's indifference at what Miri considered two very clear and cleverly joined words began to inflate inside Miri's stomach with the promise of an explosion if Mother did not respond to her words. Why would Mother not understand that Miri was communicating something important? She was sharing her vision with Mother after all.

As the next spoon was prepared and set in motion, Miri's only option was violent protest. Miri held the spoon correctly, almost to disarm her mother, and then, with well-rehearsed precision, as the spoon neared Miri's open mouth, Miri turned her head away, slung her arm and launched the spoon, complete with contents, across the length of the kitchen.

'Angels... Angels, Mama,' Miri sobbed, pointed towards Amma's shoulder again, and blurted perfectly and slowly, 'You... have... angel... face.'

There was no confusion in the four words. Miri's stare and continued pointing into the space just to the left of Mother's left shoulder, finally received the attention Miri had felt she deserved.

Mother looked towards her left shoulder where Miri was still staring and then turned to looked at her baby's face and her baby's eyes.

Children do not lie.

In that moment, call it a mother's intuition, Amma believed Miri's four words to be real, sincere and true.

First, Amma had to quickly manage the shock that Miri had joined so many words together. Then, just as instantly, Amma found herself focusing on the distress rising inside her stomach as she translated the four words, the look in Miri's eyes, and the place where she was looking and pointing, with a terrible and significant meaning.

Why would Miri say something so fantastic?

She cannot know the meaning, Amma decided. She does not know what she is saying, Amma tried to convince herself.

How can she know what an angel is? How can she see an angel?

Many explanations sped through Amma's mind and just as the sound of the spoon crashing came to halt, Amma's panic finally rested on the fear, misery and grief the words would generate in her friends and family who would hear Miri say those words with her baby voice. How would they treat Miri? This was not her land, not Korea. Miri would be accused of being sick, different, maybe even possessed. And in that moment mother decided her response. To be fair, Amma did not have much time to consider the options, only the time it took to wipe the mess at the other end of the kitchen and collect a fresh spoon.

The dread of the meaning of the words continued to grow inside Amma. But Amma was now an expert mother. She covered and camouflaged her shock so as not to frighten little Miri.

'Never say that again.' Amma reacted as calmly but firmly as she could, averting her eyes. Children can see the truth in their mother's eyes.

Then, after a fresh spoon of purée, which Miri now satisfyingly welcomed into her messy faced mouth, 'Never tell anyone else what you have told me. Let it be our secret.'

Miri was glad for the response. She listened attentively. Miri did not understand Mother's words but Miri understood her mother's voice, her face and when she eventually looked into her mother's eyes, Miri saw the fear from the echo of Miri's words and Miri did not speak those four words in that order again. At least, for another three years.

Miri learnt to grow and talk, dance and walk, and run and play. Amma and Appa were always grateful for each new morning of Miri's life, each new month of fresh breaths, and each complete year of heartbeats.

Seeing love and seeing angels became an indistinct

scene of Miri's secret life, but Miri could never be satisfied with holding secrets.

When Miri was five, she wanted to tell all her school friends about their angels. But Miri remembered her mother's words. Remembered the fear in her mother's eyes. She had to check with Mother over dinner that evening.

'I want to tell my friends. I want to tell them I see angels. I see their angels.'

Fortunately her father was at work; Amma did not react. But Amma saw the determination and confidence in Miri's eyes. And Amma, by then, had spent three years preparing for this moment.

'They will be scared of your visions, sweetheart.' Amma said her perfectly rehearsed words calmly and then, for added effect, created a fresh need to tidy up the dining table in order to clean and wipe the freshly spilled fear in her eyes. 'They will call you names, my dear. You do not want them to call you names, do you?'

Miri shook her head. 'No.'

Miri already knew what it was like to be called horrible names.

'They will call you a witch. Do you know what a witch is, sweetheart?'

She remembered her bedtime fairy stories. But they were only stories. Miri nodded, unconvinced.

'Do you remember our walk in the forest at Roncesvalles?'

'Forest?' Miri looked at her mother. They had

walked through the Forest of the Covens during a weekend trek less than two weeks before. Miri recollected the forest, the village, the church and trees. She also recollected the sweet, melting ice cream, the delightful rabbits that ran away when she approached and the bats that flew in circles above the trees in the early hours of the morning. Mother had made sure to point out the sweet-smelling herbs in the forest that women, a long time ago, used to collect to make healing potions.

'I remember, Mama. Bad people hurt the women in the forest.'

'That is right, my sweetheart. Do you remember what they did to the women? They called them witches?'

Miri looked at her mother's eyes and understood. The word was something very bad.

'They were scared of them and used to burn witches,' Mother continued. 'Do you remember the heat when you get close to the fire?'

'Ouch,' Miri pretended, putting her spoon down and clutching her hands to her chest.

'They will call you a witch. They will hurt you with fire,' Mother repeated.

Miri was so horrified at the thought. She immediately clammed up and never challenged her mother again.

Mother was satisfied.

And so Miri's gift, the love that she saw around her,

remained unseen to anyone else but her. Exactly as her mother had intended.

But Mother's disapproval of the faces of the angels, her inability to manage Miri's gift, had other unintended consequences. Or maybe they were intended. Miri came to hate her gift. Soon, she did not want to see faces, she did not want to see angels any more.

7

Eighteen

After seventeen birthdays that Miri would always remember as the happiest and confusing days of her youth, and when Miri came to realise that each birthday had been celebrated as if it would be her last, Miri enjoyed the memories of those birthdays even more.

To the surprise of all the experts, except for Miri, Miri approached her eighteenth birthday in the peak of health. Miri had accepted her body. Her body had accepted her hearts. Miri and her body had settled into a rhythm and her veins carried a hope that gently flowed into her life force.

The hospital surgeons celebrated Miri's eighteenth birthday with a day-long case conference. As well as European and international experts and researchers who had followed Miri's unique case, the hospital invited Miri and her parents to join them for the closing session in the afternoon.

Following a full day of reports, presentations and deliberations, the lead surgeon who had assisted the now retired and elderly surgeon at Miri's first surgery at her birth, and had since taken over Miri's case and treatment, welcomed the family. He reported that the assembled specialists had studied all of Miri's latest scans and tests, had read each other's reports, and their conclusion, which all had unanimously agreed, was that Miri's body exhibited every sign of calm, stability and health.

'Her charts are no different than a typical eighteen year old.' The surgeon offered the shared astonishment from the room. 'Miri's first surgery, carried out by my retired colleague eighteen years ago, was so precise, so perfect, he paved the way for Miri's survival and recovery. I have known Miri for eighteen years. My voice is breaking because I feel the relief as if Miri were my own child. We have never known a case as complicated as Miri's hearts. I express my gratitude to the skill in this room. The specialists here studied every test, performed the follow-up surgeries and cared for Miri. And to Miri's parents, you have been our inspiration. We have watched you love and care for Miri all these years. Your love and weekend treks and adventures strengthened Miri's body and freed her to heal. And to you Miri, you are an adult now. Your parents have given you the best childhood. Your childhood has known enough of hospitals and clinics and scans and tests. Go, enjoy your life.'

Having reduced the Kim family to tears, the surgeon rose. He embraced first Miri, then her parents, and finally all together. The family said their tearful thank yous and were led away to the main entrance by the surgeon.

As they parted, Amma recollected a memory and asked, 'What happened to the elderly man who performed the first surgery? We never met him again.'

'He officially retired after Miri but we kept him busy and appointed him our chief research consultant for Miri's case. He studied all of Miri's scans and tests, advised on all treatments and surgeries. We did invite him today but he could not attend; his wife is not well,' The surgeon explained before turning to Miri. The surgeon did not look at Miri's eyes, he looked down instead. 'Do not just follow a life that you have experienced with us, Miri. You are now free to create and live any life you choose. We will always be here should you need us again.'

Miri watched the surgeon step away and walk towards the conference room. Although the surgeon did not, his angel turned to look at Miri.

Miri stared at his angel for a short moment and quickly turned away. She was glad to be leaving hospitals and clinics behind her.

But in that moment she had never felt so alone. And the cause for her loneliness, she was convinced, was the angel faces.

Miri was feared.

Miri had seen angels all her life. Miri knew the intentions of everyone around her, knew the seat of their love, or lack of love. And those who looked into her eyes always saw the truth, saw themselves and never looked at her eyes ever again. Miri recognised the fear in everyone's eyes, whoever looked at her.

Without intending to, with every friend, family member, or even stranger who looked towards her, Miri knew the colour of their past, and she knew the nature of their future.

Her eyes, her vision, had driven every one of her friends away.

She had lived with the angels long enough. Now she would drive the angels away.

As she left the hospital, Miri would not just be leaving her medical history behind, she did not want to see angels any more. And somehow, in that moment, her body was listening. Her body responded. She felt a sensation, a light — was it a door? — close, inside her eyes.

She sensed a relief in her hearts.

All four hearts.

And she was glad.

And when she wept in the car on the way home, the tears came easily. Four times as many tears. Tears that streamed and were weighted with so much relief that every drop that fell onto her lap was felt with a thud that was echoed by each one of her hearts.

The tears were not for the words of the surgeon.

From the back seat, she looked at her mother and father at the front. For the first time in her life. Something was missing.

Miri could not see her mother or father's angels.

Miri had never cried so deeply before.

8

St Jean Pied de Port

The second time Miri cried so deeply, the second of three occasions in her life that she would do so, was seven years later in an *albergue* in St Jean Pied de Port, an ancient town at the foot of a pass that led through the Pyrenees mountains and follows an ancient pilgrimage route. Miri had just managed to close her eyes. But her eyes had too much pain, and her body had too many memories for sleep. This time, her tears slid down her cheeks and the bridge of her nose, and landed on the disposable pillow cover. Tears ready to be discarded in the morning. Silent tears that did not disturb the other eleven pilgrims in the room.

Eleven was also the time. Why was it, every time she looked at the time on her phone, there was pattern in the numbers? 11.11 p.m. the phone announced. Her mind and body impatiently waited for the first light of dawn that would signal the beginning of her new adventure. She was nervous. She was not ready, she had not prepared. Her first walking journey would be the Camino to Santiago Compostela.

Miri tried to calm her body. A body not used to being cocooned in a sleeping bag on a disposable sheet covering a plastic mattress. The only place her body felt any calm was when she remembered leaving the hospital the day after her eighteenth birthday, seven years ago. The moment and the last words of the surgeon had never left her. Miri had been so excited for her future that day.

Seven years of memories.

And tomorrow would be a new memory. The morning waited for her on the Pyrenees. Miri had trekked in the mountains but never walked up an entire mountain before. Miri had never trekked more than a few kilometres before. The guidebook said 28 kilometres. Would she make it to Roncesvalles? The disposable tears would not cease. But the tears were not for the uncomfortable bunk bed, or the struggle she expected to face in the morning, or the shower and bathroom she had to share with 23 pilgrims resting in the two hostel rooms. The disposable tears were for disposable love.

Being told he loved her had been enough for her. She had never explored what the words meant to him. Only now she realised she had never known or understood the meaning of his words. The words had felt the same as a feeling she now remembered as a child. The words of a lover had comforted her. Repeated in messages, so easily spoken, so easily written, so easily believed.

He was no longer in her life. So why was she leaking pain and tears? Why was she feeling so much hurt?

Miri tried to calm again hoping to sleep. Her mind returned to the surgeon once more. Why did her memory keep returning to the doorway in that hospital, to that moment?

After seven years, the memories of hospital waiting rooms and annual surgeries felt like they belonged to someone else, a Miri from another life. Had she really been so unwell as a child? Had she really been so close to death every year of her youth? She loved her parents all the more for protecting and loving her. How had her parents coped each year, not knowing if she would live or die?

Miri had given him everything. Her heart, her body, her completeness. Her every thought.

While in their last year of university, after a slow and comfortable relationship, they moved in together. And after their graduation, having secured jobs in the same city, they rented an apartment and started a life together. After five years of living with each other, she was ready to marry him, have children with him.

And then two words.

Two words on Facebook.

Two word that ripped the heart out of Miri.

"Its over"

Even the grammar was not right.

Miri blamed herself.

He did not even choose to look at her, face her, phone her, or talk with her. No, on Facebook! After so many years of loving him.

Dirt-covered "I love you" messages littered her phone and her memories. She did not want to hear those three words again.

Her parents and friends adored him. He was handsome and charming and they told her how lucky she was. She believed their words too until she realised that their words were their dreams, their desire, their fantasy, their needs and their wish to live a better life through Miri. Their dirt.

Skin-deep love.

She did not know the word love any more. This pain and anger she was feeling, she was experiencing, was not love.

Now, at least, she knew heartbreak. But the heartbreak was not for love, but broken love.

Calming, resting into the memory of the surgeon in the hospital doorway once more, the memory no longer focused on his words but the last image of the surgeon that had been caught and remained in her eye. She could not tell whether the vision was a real memory or imaginary. She could see a shadow, a face, accompany the surgeon.

Miri could not say how, but she instinctively knew the apparition was the face of an angel. And she had not thought of angels for a very long time.

Angel faces were only a vague dream. But she immediately recollected the fantasy, the childhood illusion of angel faces she had created when she was little. An imaginary world where she had lived silently and safely to dream away the endless hospital rooms and surgeries.

But the image of the angel face on the surgeon in that hospital doorway would not allow itself to be so easily discarded. A fleeting doubt rested upon her explanation. She smiled at the notion of angel faces. How creative she had been as a child, she thought. And she had not smiled in many months.

Miri decided to blame her lack of sleep on the heat. Her skin was wet, sweating. She could not breathe. The clock on her phone said 02.02 a.m.

Miri freed herself from her cocoon, the sleeping bag that was supposed to protect her from the mysteries of the night. Allowing her eyes to adjust to the warm amber street light that had entered and occupied the room, she wondered why the cold mountain breeze had refused to enter. She explored the windows only to find the curtains and windows already open; the discovery did not satisfy her.

She could have been on a beach holiday, enjoying the sand, bathing in the sea, sipping fruit cocktails. What was she doing sleeping on a bunk bed in a stuffy, sweaty, shared room at the foot of the mountain she would be climbing at dawn?

She suddenly longed for the breeze that forever flowed through her apartment. She could not breathe in that apartment either. The doors, the floor, every item in the home, especially the bed, the bathroom and the mirrors, held his memory. His scent.

She felt surrounded by a mistake. A stench of memories, imprisoned by the past five years of disposable love.

Thinking that being with her parents would help forget her misery, Miri packed a bag and booked a train. But the pollution of love would not be left behind. She could not breathe inside the complicated drama woven by her parents. Overwhelming questions, heavy silences, and masks of genuine care decorated with fussy love, which, during her confusion of loss, did not nourish her.

'The new hospital wing is opening tonight, come with us.' Her parents made an attempt to distract Miri. They had helped organise annual fundraisers for the local hospital ever since Miri was born.

But her parents had already taken her despair, and thinking it would lighten her load, made it their despair.

Miri did not want to manage their despair as well as her own.

Miri remembered the train journey to St Jean Pied de Port. She knew how she had arrived to that bunk bed. But she was confused why she had chosen to be there, to walk the Camino.

Instead, she asked why the thief of the night was stealing her sleep, stealing her air, stealing her breath. She wanted the thief to take her pain, her broken heart, the grief of her loss, grief for the love given away. The pain in her heart.

But the thief was not interested.

Did the love she had given away have such little value, she wondered?

Disposable love.

9

Roncesvalles

Four forty-four a.m. At least Miri's iPhone was not disposable. The nightmare of watching her phone falling from the top bunk and crashing onto a tiled floor ensured that Miri held her phone a little too tightly. Her hands were cramping. Sixteen minutes before her five a.m. alarm.

Miri's bladder decided not to wait for the alarm. The silent room did not welcome the creaky and wobbly metal ladder she began to descend. Miscalculating every step, she found herself holding on to the plastic mattress and squeaky bed frame for balance, further disturbing the room. Her body was surprised when her feet touched the cold floor but she was more surprised she had not dislocated an arm, broken a finger or twisted a knee. This was only the bunk bed, the Pyrenees were still waiting.

Miri used the excuse to put away her phone and pack her mochila. As soon as the mochila was packed, she gave thanks to the room that had given her sanctuary on the first night of her Camino, and as quietly as she could, but not as quietly as she hoped, she slipped away.

The stars were waiting, shining brightly,

welcoming her, she thought. But she was not alone on the cobbled street. Shadowed footsteps were already echoing through the stone lined street heading towards the mountain. She was glad not to be alone.

Stepping away from the albergue, a silhouette of a pilgrim was standing ahead of her, in the way, in the middle of the street. As she made to pass around the shadow, the image transformed into an elderly man struggling with a shoulder buckle on his mochila.

'Can I help?' Miri was surprised to hear her voice stand so sharply in the cobbled silence.

The man appeared happy for her to try to complete the buckle. Miri tried but failed to clip the two straps together.

'There should be a connector attached to the buckles. It may have fallen on my bed in the albergue. I will go back and take a look. But thank you,' the grateful pilgrim offered with a soft Spanish accent. She watched him head back to his albergue.

What will the weather be like?

Will the mountain be as steep as the book describes?

I did not prepare for this mountain, I did not prepare for an 800km walk.

I am scared. Scared of not making it up the mountain, scared of not making it to Santiago.

The rucksack feels heavy. There is too much in the mochila. My boots are not comfortable.

Miri's mochila was already full of countless

anxieties.

Reaching a bridge at the foot of the town, Miri paused and closed her eyes to listen to the fresh flowing river. She breathed the sound, as deeply as she could, to calm her senses. Walking through the narrow street again, the scent of baking bread teased her anxieties. Miri immediately thought of a café con leche and a freshly baked croissant, but the bars were still closed. Reaching the end of the street, she felt a new freshness as the cold mountain air rushed towards her and washed the café con leche away from her mind and the sleep away from her skin, cleansing her worries. She had arrived at the foot of the mountain. She was on the Camino. Miri calmed and returned the smile to the night.

She did not see, and she did not know that she had stopped seeing, but the Camino smiled too.

Stars continue to shine, but when the eyes no longer see them, stars are forgotten. Miri had forgotten the stars. As she began the climb, she stared at the stars as if seeing them for the first time. Had she forgotten the world too?

She sensed the wet dew exploring her skin, and wondered how she could have forgotten that sensation too.

As the path became steeper and her breathing faltered, she wondered, what am I doing here? Her mind began to challenge her decision.

She looked at the steeper climb ahead and the

darkness inside took hold once more.

Should I be walking alone?

The sun has not risen. I cannot see any arrows. Am I going the right way?

Will I be safe?

Can I do this?

What am I doing here?

The steep climb did not abate and Miri struggled to breathe. The question of why remained. What was she was doing on the Pyrenees, on the Camino, torturing herself? This was only the first day. The first few hours. She eventually reached the top of the steep section but the mountain still loomed ahead.

One by one, pilgrims began to catch up and pass her. She had no time to look at the spectacularly decorated street light night views of the valley below, she only wanted to breathe.

When the sun rose, the mist began to lift revealing a painted green and yellow valley and, for now, a spotless light-blue sky.

Miri's body felt free. Felt free to suffer. Felt free to forget her past, let go of her grief. But Miri's mind was not so quick to let go.

Four steep and painful hours later, Miri reached a viewpoint where she unclipped her rucksack and let herself fall to the ground hoping to appease her complaining, thumping hearts.

The drumming in her chest slowed and the guidebook in the side pocket of the mochila conveniently fell to the ground to distract her. Finding the page with the map and elevation of the day's climb, she saw a symbol for a rest area and gave herself comfort that the first and only mountain bar and coffee stop was not too far away. She looked towards the top of the mountain as if to check the mountain was real. And then she looked below to check that she really had been climbing it. She was shocked at the height already climbed. Her hearts and her breathing were calming but she could also sense protest from every part of her body.

The mountain had a voice too. The language of mountains is difficult to read. But in that moment Miri knew that the mountain welcomed her. The top of the mountain was waiting for her.

Her hearts still heavy and recovering, Miri's attention was drawn towards a group of pilgrims laughing loudly behind her. Her mind felt good to hear joy and she turned her head towards them. She did not immediately recognise a man putting on his rucksack and leaving the group. He looked familiar.

'He is 82 years old, look at him climb!' Two young pilgrims were excitedly chatting with each other.

Staring at the departing pilgrim, she realised he was the same old man from the morning in St Jean Pied de Port. The man who had been struggling with the buckle outside the albergue.

'How... *when* did he pass me?' Miri stammered, feeling humbled and ashamed of her complaining body. She made herself a promise in that moment.

'At the age of 82, I am going to walk this mountain, this journey, the whole Camino.'

Having realised the words of her new commitment, her shame, Miri smiled. She sensed an energy, a message. The Camino was introducing itself. The mountain was talking to her. She smiled at the mountain.

And maybe it was the smile that carried Miri's body up to and through the pass of Roland where she let her imagination wander to ancient legends of giants, kings, invaders, battles and Roman legions who marched upon the path. Then she grew excited at the thought of bandits laying in wait and the Knights Templar rescuing her from a bandit attack.

But it was not Miri's smile, it was the mountain that carried Miri. The mountain knew Miri. The Camino had been waiting for Miri, expecting her.

Fortunately there were no bandits on the road to Roncesvalles, and most certainly no knights. But the queue for a bed in the albergue in Roncesvalles was long. An army of pilgrims waiting to invade northern Spain. Miri was allocated one of the last beds on the top floor of the main building. The Dutch *voluntarios* were stretched with the day's tasks and explained that five hundred pilgrims were sleeping in the monastery that night.

Miri's smile remained broad when she climbed and then collapsed on her top bunk after a hot, healing shower. The relief. Her hearts slowed. Her breathing relaxed. She had made it to Roncesvalles. Had she really walked 28km? The guidebook insisted she had. Miri felt an achievement, strong, unlike the very tired pilgrim in the bunk bed below who, still in his walking clothes, had fallen on his mattress and was already snoring. Miri laughed at the snoring and was glad to have brought a pack of ear plugs with her. And then she laughed again as she congratulated herself for managing to shower in spite of a shower button that would only allow one minute of showering with each press.

Miri's eyes closed well before the ten p.m. automated dormitory lights. Trying not to remember what she was walking away from, Miri's mind disappeared inside a labyrinth of denial and somewhere inside that maze, Miri recognised a tortured soul. Did she really believe that walking the Camino would ease her pain, her fear?

Fear? A terrible word to carry, Miri thought. And Miri did not want to carry more. The mochila was already full.

And fear of what? Fear of whom?

Fear to love again? The pain of love?

Fear of love?

But love cannot be torn from life.

The cool air flowing through the large dormitory made tonight's bed more comfortable than the night before. Her eyes closed, Miri allowed her mind to wander through the views and sensations of the day. But her attention eventually settled on the small paper form all pilgrims had been asked to complete while queuing for a bed at the albergue. She had already filled in the form and collected her credential from St Jean Pied de Port. The passport would allow her access to a bed in all the *albergues* along the Camino. She could not understand why she had to complete another form. There was one question on this paper that remained in her eye and kept her from dreaming. The question asked which religion she was. There were three options: Catholic, Protestant and Other. Miri did not hesitate and ticked "Other".

'I am the "other". I have been the "other" all my life.'

10

Mountain of Forgiveness

The light that lit the Camino through the forest in Roncesvalles in the early hours of the morning was not the sun or the moon or the morning stars, but Miri's iPhone.

Being alone under the canopy-draped black darkness did not scare Miri. She felt grateful that the phone was fully charged and for the light that lit the way allowing her to navigate the forest growth without tripping. She felt grateful to the forest for welcoming her, for the pilgrims who were sharing the journey with her, for the comfort she felt stepping through the invisible silence of the forest. Was it the forest? Or was it the Camino? Miri's dinner table the evening before had pilgrims from Japan, Germany, Holland and Italy. She could not describe the surprise of being surrounded by pilgrims from so many nations. Languages she could not understand. But she sensed her joy in the experience.

And when Miri saw the early dawn light fall into a forest clearing ahead, Miri slowed, switched off her torch and enjoyed the light filling her eyes. The forest appeared to unwrap the Camino for Miri. A present of fresh morning green tinged with a sunrise orange.

Miri almost missed a signboard amongst the trees on her left as she entered the clearing, but when she saw the words, she was intrigued. A good excuse to pause and breathe the first light.

A strange place to have a signboard. The light was not yet strong enough to read the small writing but it felt good to shine the torch on something other than the ground. As soon as she read the name of the forest a wave of emotions and recollections began to pour into her mind. She had just walked through the Forest of Covens.

She did not know how long she had stood in front of the sign, reading the words, but the invitation to return to the Camino arrived with the sound of rustling steps of approaching pilgrims.

The short walk leading out of the forest into Burguete also led to a second invitation of the dawn. A brightly lit coffee shop coupled with the aroma of fresh baking breads suggesting Miri sit, enjoy the morning, the moment, and remember.

But even as Miri ordered her morning tradition and settled outside under the fresh dawn-sprinkled air, the name of both the forest and the village, Burguete, unlocked another door to one of Miri's childhood bedtime stories. The "Forest of Covens". Reading the word 'witch' on the forest sign set free a long-forgotten pain held inside her. An embarrassing pain she had not felt for a very long time. She knew the word too well. She knew the mortifying feeling inside the word. And when her hearts tried to step into the details of the memory, the locked memories of her youth found no key. More doors to open.

Coffee is a mystery.

For Miri, coffee always unlocked the mystery of the morning. As Miri enjoyed her still warm, freshly baked croissant and café con leche, the best coffee that the Camino — maybe even Spain — had to offer, Miri felt a coffee-scented calming energy rapidly rise inside her and flow into her hearts and fill her mind. The mystery of the coffee today. Her body felt strong, awake. Miri stood, lifted her mochila and made it comfortable around her and stepped forward into a sense of a past that she did not yet feel ready to discover. A passing hotel sign with the name "Hemingway" offered a fleeting distraction, he must have liked the Spanish café con leche too, she thought, but when she saw the church with the trees lined in three rows of four, she also saw the women tied to posts where the trees were growing and her eyes began to water and the memory of her mother's witch stories made her walk even faster. She was glad to see the yellow arrow heading away from the church. She did not want more memories to add to the troubles she was running from.

But it was too late. The mystery of today's coffee had found another key. But the door had yet to open.

Miri walked with the sunrise behind her, shadows in front of her. She did not look at the sun. The sun was the past. She did not stop. Not even to amaze at the swooping, frolicking morning bats that swooped and danced above her as she passed through the tree-lined avenue out of Burguete. She began a dance because the place felt familiar, but the dance only lasted four steps. The dance of the bats was even more familiar.

Miri quickened her pace. *Where are you rushing to?* the Camino asked. Miri heard the words but did not want to listen. She did not even listen to the sunlit colours of the valley when they welcomed her. She felt comforted walking through the forest. When the forest ended and another village arrived, she longed for the forest again. And in the next forest, she was surprised to find a small pilgrim memorial nestled amongst the trees. Here she paused to remember and pay her respects to the fallen. "From Japan," she read. Sitting without removing her mochila, Miri balanced herself on a cut tree trunk neatly placed next to the memorial. Quenching her thirst, Miri wondered if anyone would remember her, or her Camino. When the fast-flowing river in Zubiri tried to answer her and invited her to dip her aching feet, Miri did not listen. She did not know where she would sleep that night but she also knew she did not want her body to stop moving. If her body stopped, her mind would feel her aching body and she knew she would find her aching hearts inside.

Miri walked into the early evening. Finally she stopped at the convent at Zabaldika, and not because her legs screamed but because the church bell rang and the voice of the bell reached her.

Miri's shoulders and back ached with the weight of the rucksack. The rucksack felt heavier. Her blistered feet screamed. She seemed to have collected more burdens and yet she was supposed to let go of them.

The gentle way of the nuns of Zabaldika, their simple food, their calming words, their singing voices, their evening pilgrim's prayer, invited Miri to pause, to breathe. For a moment at least. And the nuns asked for nothing in return. Not even a donation.

Wrapped in her sleeping bag, she tried to invite words that would begin to console her broken hearts. But the words did not approach, or maybe the healing was too far away.

Her wordless world of feelings had sealed her mind and her body. Her emotions did not want the burden of labels. Her mind just wanted her body to weep, collapse, feel. Her soul was resisting. Why was her mind resisting? What did she not want to feel, to remember, to know?

Miri's mind or body, she could not say which, woke in the middle of the night. Unable to sleep, she wanted to leave the undeserved comfort of the bed, the undeserved care and love the nuns had showered upon her. Why would she not deserve their love?

There had been a music and rhythm in her childhood, Miri suddenly remembered, she was sure. Where had it gone? Why could she not feel or hear the music of her heartbeats any more?

What was the truth she was running from?

When did she stop dancing?

As she lay on a top bunk, Miri's feet were not satisfied with the rest, or the night, and demanded to feel the earth underneath. Her body needed to feel the rhythm of her walking and the freshness of the air. The Camino seemed to have already reached inside her and whatever the Camino was, something inside wanted the Camino to take her away from the maze of chaos in her mind.

But the Camino had no intention to take a pilgrim away from chaos. The Camino brings you closer to chaos.

Opening her eyes, Miri could see the silhouettes of the trees through the window. A clear night sky. The stars appeared to be waiting for her too. Why would the stars be waiting for her, her soul? A soul she was still looking for?

Stealthy footsteps and a light on the other side of the dormitory door signalled the beginning of the pilgrim's day. An early riser was heading to the bathroom. Miri checked her phone. It was 4.44 a.m. Time to leave.

The cold night air and starlit sky were Miri's nourishing companions, not the bed, or the room. Her feet already made friends with the earth. The earth had been her only constant these last few days. The journey, her Camino at least, had only just begun and it was the earth, at each step, lifting her back up again with a touch, an embrace, a care, a tenderness, holding her from falling into the empty void of all her feelings.

The earth had always been there. When had she forgotten the healing of the earth under her feet?

The fresh darkness held no sound, no words, only a scent of freedom and a gentle blue light while stroking Miri's waking skin. And Miri's elated feet, quickly finding the yellow arrow pointing towards Pamplona, stepped quickly towards the bulls.

Miri could not tell, was she beginning the day? Or was she following the day?

Miri was carrying a new feeling, a new sensation. The voices of the nuns of Zabaldika had reached inside her. No one arrives in Zabaldika and leaves empty hearted.

Miri did not stop for the sunrise and she only smiled at San Fermín in Pamplona. She did not wait to run with the bulls but she did wade through the madness of the night's empty discarded beer cans and bottles. Even the loud music, courting her to enter the early morning dancing bars, did not invade her spirit. She watched and smiled with the dancing bull-worshippers. She loved dancing, but not for the bulls, she thought. She walked through and out of Pamplona, glad to leave the noise and mess behind, and wondering if some of the noise and mess inside her would be left behind.

The soft, freshly mowed grass on the university grounds caressed her feet gently. Climbing the hill to Cizur Menor where the flag of the Templars of Malta proudly waved over an ancient church, Miri might have stopped at the albergue but her legs did not wish to. Miri meandered through the fields and gentle hills eventually reaching a hamlet, just before the Mountain of Forgiveness, where she collapsed at a bar with an albergue.

Except to fill her water bottle from the fresh water fountains along the way, Miri, again, had not rested. Her body was screaming again.

Having dropped her mochila outside the bar, Miri paid for a bed and a café con leche, and found an empty table inside. All the tables were empty.

'We are still cleaning the rooms. I will show you your bed when the room is ready,' the owner explained.

Miri's eyes were immediately drawn to a small poster on the wall behind her, as was probably intended.

"Welcome to today.

Another day, another chance.

Feel free to change."

Maybe the sign, not the words, made her smile.

But she did smile.

And the smile healed the moment. Healed her aches. Her body, resting now, enjoyed the smile too. And the moment led to more smiles. And Miri's smile led to a new calm. The mountain of forgiveness is waiting for me, Miri smiled with hope this time.

Miri slept deeply that night. And she would have slept for longer had it not been for the very creaky bed above her. A particularly heavy movement of the body on the mattress above instantly transformed into a whine, groan and finally the shriek of the bed caused Miri's eyes to open. Miri smiled to the morning light as it gently knocked on the windows. *It's OK.* She calmed her body. *I hear you.*

Miri's body did not need to hear the iPhone alarm any more. At 05.05 a.m., she collected her mochila, sleeping bag and pillow case, and quietly made her way out of the dormitory room. Finding a space in the empty bar to change, pack, and ready for the day, she was surprised to have already found a new and comforting, morning routine. How many days had she walked? Not many, and yet she had lost count.

Miri was surprised to find her feet enjoying the caress as they slid into their boots. Her blisters had given way, finally. Miri was surprised again as she recognised the new comfort, the embrace of her mochila when she wrapped the belt around her. And she had not felt comforted in a while.

With a final check that nothing was left behind or fallen on the floor, a moment of insecurity enveloped her and she felt compelled to creep back upstairs to her empty bed, aided by her iPhone torch, to check that nothing had been left on the mattress, fallen on the floor or left hanging from the bed. She returned to the main door of the albergue, quietly satisfied.

With her hand on the door handle, her eye caught the sign on the wall from the evening before. She had to take a photo. In that moment, the words of the sign, not the air outside, were more important.

Thank you, she appeared to say to the sign and the albergue.

Doors to albergues are one way. Once you walk through the door at five thirty a.m., the door closes behind and locks itself. Albergues are secure. There is no way back in.

Miri was already learning not to look back.

The early morning footpath was dark but not as dark as the forest had been in Roncesvalles. A stretch of overgrown, rocky, and uneven uphill footpath made use of Miri's torch, the light focusing on one lit spot at her feet to make sure she did not trip or fall.

'If only life were this simple,' Miri laughed.

Just as the jealous sun made its first attempts to challenge the smartphone, Miri neared the end of the climb. Reaching the top of a mountain is always a relief. On this mountain, a very particular dawn welcome was waiting.

Miri was instantly mesmerised by a row of life-sized black metal sculptures of medieval pilgrims and animals, a small caravan heading to Santiago, walking along the Camino. A donkey, no, two. A horse. Miri counted twelve life-sized people including children, and a beautiful dog. Flags on tall poles announced their journey to everyone they encountered.

Miri could not take her eyes off two young girls with flowing, tied hair. She saw her youth in the girls, in their hair. They are happy, she thought. She remembered her childhood. A time of unbreakable love.

Before the love that breaks hearts.

The sculptures. Pilgrims. Who were they? A family? A group of friends? Pilgrims brought together by fate? The thought took her mind to another past, to the beginning of all pasts. A time of kings who left the first footsteps for the very first Camino.

As a young girl, ever since her father had accidentally read to her a story of the first ancient kings, and the story told that these ancient kings could speak with angels and spirits, she had cherished a secret obsession with these kings.

Accidentally, because Amma made sure the story was never repeated ever again.

Miri never told her father, nor anyone, why she was interested in this story. No one would have understood anyway. When she grew older and knew how, she began her own research. She explored every reference, every ancient scripture she could find that told of the first ancient kings and their relationship with angels. She found a reference to a story of angels on the Mountain of Oaths. Soon the interest waned and now she understood that these stories had been the source of her childhood fascination with angels and the fantasies and faces she had created.

Miri was alone, free, standing on the very top of a mountain ridge. Who was she? The colours of the changing dawn and the rising flowing mist behind the front two pilgrim silhouette sculptures brought Miri back to the present. Who were they? Were they lovers?

Miri fleetingly wondered what it would be like to walk the Camino with a lover. Miri raised her arms above her, to the sky, thanking her god, the earth, the mountain, the Camino, every spirit, every angel that was listening, for the moment, for her existence, her life and presence in this moment. She thanked the artist who had created a perfect sculpture for this perfect place. She listened to the spirit of the artist's inspiration that, in the whispering shadows of the morning light on this Mountain of Forgiveness, invited Miri to remove her mochila and stay for a while. Miri sat at the stone monolith. Tears she had tried so hard to run away from, to hide behind, to walk away on the mountain after St Jean Pied de Port, had not been left behind, had not left her, and now, here, in front of the metal pilgrims, the salty drops found a rusty leak in her soul. Tears eager to escape and remain on the Mountain of Forgiveness. Tears ready to let Miri go, to escape. To heal. To forgive.

Miri wept her silent heartache.

Miri knew to allow her tears to talk, to be.

Miri had allowed herself to become a soulless metal pilgrim of life. The tears were telling her to look, and to feel, to unlock a lost part of her.

The sculptures in front of her were unable to look and to feel. But they touched the lost feeling inside her.

And Miri was ready to feel, and to find herself again.

She felt. For the first time in a long time, she felt.

And the feelings came as words that were held inside each tear. Words that had been frozen, waiting deep inside, hiding her cold soul, hiding her hearts, were now thawing and leaking out inside each tear. And she felt the sense of every word, every tear.

Broken hearts find words.

Nothing is random, nothing a coincidence. Normally packed deep inside the mochila, Miri reached for her diary and pen which today rested in a zip lock bag on an outer pocket, as if knowing this moment.

The Bull too knew this moment would come. The Bull waited.

Miri opened the wordless pages. The tears wrote the words.

11

Miri's Diary

"Yesterday, I felt the dawn air stand still in the forest of Roncesvalles, shy of my approach, shy of knowing my mystery. Shy of my memory.

Today, on this mountain of forgiveness, I feel the morning air caress me. Kiss my skin. The feel of the kiss takes my breath away.

I want to be free of my burdens.

I want to feel again. Feel the world again.

I want to feel my hearts again.

I want to write about the air on the mountain,

The air that I have walked through.

The air that I cut in half as I walked.

I want to write about the feel of the earth when it lifts my feet and keeps me from sinking.

The sun that bounces from my hair, reminding me to breathe.

I want to find the words that describe the blue frozen world that I step into every morning, or is it pink? I cannot tell.

I want a word that describes the bird that greets and wakes me when the dawn light creeps through the hostel window.

I want a word that describes the joy of the tree that holds the waking bird.

I am tired of the world of excuses, reasons, heartbreaks, gossip and egos.

I only want to feel this moment and describe this moment.

But I cannot.

It is too far from any word I know.

But I feel the moment.

A sketch of this moment remains inside me even when the moment has passed.

I feel the sacred ideas that represent this moment, every moment, but the words are not there.

I want to describe the breeze on this mountain that is flowing through my hair, stroking my skin and lifting my scarf, as if I am the artwork.

The strong light of the sun battling through the clouds to reach me as if with an endless kiss.

I remember the kiss of one I loved. A love I feel no more.

A kiss that made me forget the light around me.

I want to write about the light around me.

Not the sun.

But the light.

The light is trapped inside the air that I breathe.

The light lifts me, guides me towards my new day,

To a place where I no longer need to see.

A place where I am free to feel.

I will erase the sketch of my life's feelings that was

before and what might happen next.

Inside the painting that is this mountain.

I must find the word.

But I want my words to become the beacon that will lead me to this memory again.

To become the air that I am breathing when I live this memory again.

To be the earth that I am touching now, on this mountain.

Can a mountain forgive? Can I forgive?

I want the birdsong to enter and decorate my soul, a soul that beats with my hearts, hearts that I cannot yet hear. Hearts I have forgotten to hear.

I have forgotten to dance.

I want to feel the word that will describe the way I dance. I used to dance.

I cannot see myself and yet the pool left behind by the invisible rain in the night has seen me. The water has seen me approaching and creates another me.

I am not the only one in the pool, my shadow is there too. I become the reflection, another.

The mountain grass is moving and dancing with the wind. The mountain is waking to the sun. The tears of the night have been collected by the flowers and the grass and the earth.

My hearts thirst to be covered by the teardrops of the fading night.

Will there ever be one word that describes the colours and sensations of today's dawn? The light in this dawn? A dawn like no other in the past or in the dawns to come?

Will there ever be a word that describes how the stars became the light of the night and are no more? Or how the moon becomes the beacon of the night?

Maybe the light is not a word, but a lighthouse to the spirits. To the angels I once saw as a child.

Am I listening to the light? Or am I listening to my soul? Or am listening to the spirits?

I am on the Camino.

For the first time I understand the Camino is not words.

It is feeling.

It lasts.

It captures.

It holds.

It lasts.

It leaves a gasp of air as you enter a moment, leaving behind despair, and pain. And yet, it is torture when you leave the moment.

For it is only a moment.

I thank this moment. The air in this moment that I breathe has become an infinite embrace of the hearts and my soul.

With each tear I write, and with each word I sense the darkness is passing. The morning stars that were my companions this morning, surrounding me, touching me with their light, a light that held the spirit of the universe, a moment I was united with the universe, is fading.

In a moment, I will stand on this mountain of forgiveness.

When I stand, my feet will lift away from the earth to walk.

What is forgiveness?

The word is still missing.

Is it a void?

It might be a hope.

Has the void always been inside me?

Is it the closed world I grasp tightly with my left hand? That world I was born with.

What is in my hand?

The sun is rising now. The sunlight is touching me, warming me, waking my skin, embracing me and will, in a moment, forget me.

What have I lost in order to gain this thought?

I want a word that will make the world forget me."

12

The Camino

"I want a word that will make the world forget me."

On the Mountain of Forgiveness, Miri's body felt bare, her heart felt empty.

Hari heard the cry. The cry of despair. And when a heart feels despair, the soul calls the Burden Collector.

Miri did not know, but there was one other who had been waiting for this moment, who knew the coming of this moment. A bull. A very ancient bull. A bull who had been preparing Miri all of her life for this one moment. The Bull had only one purpose: to protect Miri.

And the Bull also knew that when this moment of despair arrived, only one place would protect her from Hari. Miri had to be on the Camino.

Hari also had a purpose. Hari did not know time, only moments. And when Hari heard Miri's call from the Mountain of Forgiveness, he was in a hospital just after the moment of Miri's birth, staring at her frozen hand. Hari had already decided that he wanted the force inside Miri's hand for himself.

But while Hari had now learnt that he could not approach a newborn, in this new moment that called to him, Miri was now an adult and had now invited the

Burden Collector of her own free will. The beacon of despair had been lit. And the beacon gave permission for the Collector of Burdens to approach Miri and the hand that held the force, the mystery.

Hari looked towards the new moment, and sensed the significance. The mystery of the universe, grasped within the palm of Miri's left hand, was waiting. But he also sensed something new, an energy around him, or was it within him?

And when he approached the adult Miri, the energy grew stronger. Hari could see Miri. But he could not see the Mountain of Forgiveness. He did not know where she was.

What was the emptiness around her? Not emptiness, but this sensation he had not felt before. Hari did not know the Camino. Hari could not see the Camino at all. Because Hari did not know forgiveness and he did not know love.

Hari was confused.

Hari had never been confused before.

What energy was this that would not let him pass or approach Miri?

The Bull also looked.

If every being has a spirit that protects, then Miri's spirit was a bull. A particularly large bull with four horns. Miri was in Spain, she had four hearts, so why not?

The moment when Miri called the Collector of Burdens had arrived and passed. A moment that could not be undone. The Bull waited.

A moment with an end, a beginning, and a consequence.

The Bull, being an expert in protecting, did not know of the energy or mystery or what was contained in the palm of Miri's hand. And the Bull, a spirit who had also taken the oath, would serve and protect Miri. The Bull did not understand time. But the Bull knew danger. The Bull knew of a moment to come. And when the moment came, Miri would face danger. Not an ordinary danger, but a danger from the time of the ancient kings. A time on the Mountain of Oaths. A danger beyond the understanding of the Bull.

But the Bull had no need to understand.

The Bull had brought Miri to the only space where Miri would be safe and protected.

The Camino.

Not much in the universe is unknown.

And this moment, to Hari's surprise, did not, as yet, have a consequence.

But Hari had an intention. An intention with a consequence that would wrap the entire universe.

Hari intended to destroy everything associated with the word love, the very purpose of life. He would destroy time.

How Hari knew what he intended to do, he did not yet know. For wanting to know was still behind him.

Miri, also, did not yet know why she had ordered a mochila. At the time she had wondered about a beach holiday. She imagined a blue sky over a blue sea, white sand, the sound of gentle waves, a fruit cocktail on the table and a book in her hand. Instead she found herself ordering a mochila, walking sticks and a sleeping bag from the internet.

Why choose discomfort, the pain of walking and climbing mountains instead of the towel on the beach? She could not say.

But her body knew.

And she knew the terrible grief of the loss of love.

She had read two books about the Camino, talked with friends who had walked the Camino, listened to her mother who had always dreamed of walking the way, they even watched the movie together.

'My wish to walk the Camino began when you were born.' Amma remembered the surgeon's words.

'Come with me,' Miri encouraged. 'We walk together.'

'I will slow you down. Go.' Her mother already understood. 'You need to be alone.'

Miri was relieved. She wanted to be alone. To understand the love she had given and received. And the heartbreak. She needed to understand the pain of the heartbreak. Miri needed to free herself from that past relationship. She needed to hear her hearts again. To feel the rhythm again. Somehow, Miri knew — how she knew she could not say — that the Camino was the place for her to feel again. To collect her feelings, past and present. Where she could walk alone and put her present into the past.

Miri requested a month's leave from work.

'I need this time!'

Her boss needed her at work but understood too. Miri was stubborn. If she did not grant her the leave, she knew Miri would resign and not return the next day.

The Bull could do no more. Even protectors have their limits.

The novels, the movie, the friends, the boss, the internet shopping site, Miri's mother. In fact there were many more yellow arrows that Miri did not see or grasp. The Bull had painted all of them, pointing each towards the Camino.

But only Miri could make the choice to take the first step on the Camino and be. The Bull could not lead her hearts, could not carry her soul. The Bull did not know life. But the Bull did know that the Miri's first step on the Camino would touch the footsteps of the ancient kings. The first kings who spoke with angels.

The guidebook had played its part too. Miri began poring over the maps and absorbing the descriptions of each day's walks as soon as the book arrived. The distances were long, too long, she thought. After staring at the graphs with the hill gradients, the graph of the first day in particular, Miri almost gave up on the idea of the Camino and retreated again to the idea of the beach on the Spanish south coast. 'I will walk a few days,' she decided. 'If it is too difficult, I will book a train to the south, to the beach.' She felt better.

When the train ticket was booked and the mochila packed, the Protector still waited. When Miri was on the train to St Jean Pied de Port sitting next to a silent family, silent parents with a silent daughter the same age as Miri, the Bull continued to wait. The silent family had Camino mochilas too. Scallop shells. Miri smiled a nervous smile at them as she inspected their mochilas. Smaller than hers. She panicked. She had brought too much. The father nodded his acknowledgement to Miri. They would be walking on the Camino too. Miri was glad they did not try to speak with her. She was not in the mood for conversation.

Only when Miri entered the faint dawn light bouncing off the cobbled street as she closed the door of the hostel behind her and stepped upon the ancient path to begin her pilgrimage, her Camino, was the Bull satisfied.

Hari could see Miri but he could not approach her. He felt the moment seize him, capture him, confuse him, wrap around him, trap him. Hari was inside a moment, but the moment would not carry him to Miri.

Hari did not understand, for Hari did not know the Camino.

Hari was a spirit.

And spirits do not know love.

The Bull did not know love either. But the Bull knew how to protect. The Bull knew the Camino.

13

Puente la Reina

'Take one stick, I have two!'

A pilgrim, having seen Raphael's struggle, called and slowed to walk with him on the descent from the Mountain of Forgiveness. Raphael was grateful to his new walking companion, an 82-year-old pilgrim from Spain, he quickly discovered. The walking stick helped with Raphael's balance, instantly took away the stress on his knees and reduced the intense shooting pain on his right knee. He would buy a pair of sticks in Puente la Reina, Raphael decided.

The pilgrim remained with him through the entire steep, slippery and gravel-filled descent. Raphael had not even though to ask his name. His companion had not volunteered it. But, very cleverly, as Raphael would decide after the descent, this wonderful pilgrim had taken his mind away from his struggling knees by sharing stories.

'Thank you for walking with me. You are full of stories. I love that you are walking the Camino and experiencing this world. I cannot believe that your family was so worried for you and telling you to stay at home; you are fitter than me! And I cannot believe that all the coffee shops in every village we have passed have been closed this morning. I need coffee. I think the pain in my knee just needs a café con leche,' Raphael laughed.

'The stick has helped. But I will stop at the next albergue to rest my knees for the night,' he confessed.

'The next town, according to my book, is called Puente la Reina. Do you remember the town from last year?'

'It's all a blur,' Raphael laughed, trying to remember. Raphael had walked all the way to Santiago from St Jean Pied de Port the previous year; he was shocked that he could not remember the towns. His knees had been fine the last year. He could not understand why they hurt this year. His left knee was hurting more than the right. One spot on the left part of the knee was troubling him with shooting pains.

'But I do remember that chimney.' Raphael pointed towards a very tall, slim factory chimney rising out of the old town in the valley. 'There was a huge stork's nest on top of that chimney with a mother and a baby. No nest and no storks this year.'

'No stork's nest this year but you are back on the Camino.'

The pilgrim might have been a poet, Raphael thought.

'Something inside you is unfinished, the Camino has invited you again.' The pilgrim shared his wisdom. 'You must have asked yourself why you returned,' the pilgrim probed.

Raphael thought about the question. The question he would have preferred, and was frequently asked, was why he was walking the Camino. In the absence of an immediate reply to this new question, he answered as if in reply to the question he was already used to.

'My grandmother lives on the Camino. She lives in the Meseta. I am visiting her. Again!' Raphael tried to smile his diversion away.

Visiting his grandma was only an excuse. He could have taken a bus. But while the reply always satisfied those who asked, his new companion was not so easily satisfied.

'But why walk a second time?' and immediately apologised. 'I am sorry. No need to answer. There is a lot going on in my head too.'

The question was not unfamiliar. Raphael had asked himself the same question when he landed at Biarritz airport and every day since. Without an explanation, he felt conflicted and confused. There was something, a feeling, Raphael had been carrying inside him from his last Camino. And Raphael was not very good with feelings.

Raphael had harvested a powerful, deep and new sensation from the Camino the previous year. The feeling stayed with him on his return to Milan. He guarded the sensation preciously for many months after the Camino, only to find it slowly erode and dissolve when the daily rhythms of his life became more important.

The sensation he had felt on the Camino, a powerful indescribable feeling he carried from the previous year, had completed him, inside and out. And no matter what he did in Milan, he had never felt that way again. What was the feeling? Could it be joy? Had he really never experienced joy before? And when, after a few months, the feeling only appeared as a fleeting touch of a memory, the emotion of a remnant sensation always moved him, occasionally releasing an uncontrolled and gentle, silent tear. He was not good with tears either. How could he describe these feelings to other pilgrims when he could not understand them himself?

'I think I understand,' the pilgrim helped. Raphael had not said anything. 'I can hear your words.'

'I think I came back for the Spanish café con leche and freshly baked croissants,' Raphael joked. He had to sit down soon.

'I can smell fresh baking! I think your coffee shop is arriving.'

They both explored the cobbled pedestrian *calle* stretching in front of them with anticipation that the activity ahead may suggest an open bar.

Raphael was relieved when he stepped in front of the bakery and coffee shop, and it was open. Raphael unclipped and dropped his mochila while inviting his new friend, 'Join me. Let me buy you a coffee.' Raphael returned the walking stick.

'Too early for me. I will stop a little later.'

Raphael was slightly disappointed. But he knew everyone had their own rhythm and had to make their own camino.

'Thank you.' Raphael tried to express his gratitude. The words did not seem enough.

'The Camino always gives you what you need. Stop and rest. I am sure we will meet again. We have a long way to go.'

'One thing, if I may. What next? After the Camino I mean. What will be your next adventure?'

The pilgrim paused and smiled. 'A Harley Davidson!' he instantly offered. 'But the problem is, they will not give me a licence. They say I am too old!' And with an infectious laugh, he stepped away towards the Royal Bridge.

Raphael always amazed at the endless inspiring people he was meeting on the Camino. He stepped into the café bakery and filled himself with aromas of fresh baking breads and pastries, instantly entering his small bubble of heaven.

Even in heaven, knees hurt. Raphael tried to massage a knee while waiting for his order. He should have massaged his knees after the steep descent into Roncesvalles, he thought. The pain had begun in Roncesvalles. Today's uneven path, loose rocks down the second descent had not been kind to his left knee.

Collecting his comfort from the counter, he limped to the only free chair at the only vacant table by the door. He paused briefly to enjoy the satisfied sounds of the full coffee shop before surrendering to the coffee dipped piece of fresh croissant. At the precise moment of the first bite of his croissant, he could not help but notice a face at the other end of the coffee shop staring directly at him. He immediately knew she was a pilgrim. She was wearing the Camino uniform. His first thought was that they had already met on the Camino, why was she looking at him? So he looked at her too and attempted a smile, just in case, trying to remember where they might have walked together or passed each other. But the smile was not returned and she looked away. He did not recollect her. She was sitting alone. He looked towards her again to check. This time she appeared unsettled and began to get ready to leave.

Returning to his croissant and just as Raphael was about to take his second bite of the coffee dipped croissant, which can be a little messy and unpredictable sometimes, he found that she was looking at him again, more intensely, and this time their eyes met. The feeling that rose in him made him almost forget the warm comfort entering his lips, because a deeper comfort filled his eyes. He immediately convinced himself that hers was the most beautiful face he had ever seen. Of course, he had experienced that same feeling twice before, once at a Milano metro station. He was getting off the metro and a vision brushed against him as she was getting onto the train. The second time his heart had stopped was at a checkout in a Conad supermarket, again in Milan. Both times the women had, almost entirely, ignored him and yet he could not let go of the sight of them.

Love at first sight, twice before. 'At first sight' is all they were, and, probably, were ever intended to be.

But unlike the other two moments, a smile from the face of the woman at the other end of the coffee shop reached him. Raphael's body caught the smile and suddenly he found himself aching in his stomach.

The way she looked at him, she was looking inside him, into his very soul. He wanted her to keep looking and describe everything she was seeing. He wanted to tell her every feeling inside him, everything he felt just by looking at that beautiful smile.

He was already embarrassed and now even a little confused. His mind seemed to explode. Pilgrims go crazy when they explode.

There was still a piece of freshly baked croissant in his hand and some more in his mouth and probably some more dripping down his quick-dry technical trekking shirt. But he could not help but watch the perfect vision as she stood and began to walk across the coffee shop towards him. Was she coming to sit with him? But her face had changed. Raphael recognised pain and upset on her face as she hurried past him, avoiding his gaze. Raphael turned to see her rush through the open door, collect her rucksack and step away into the street. Why had he not said hello when she passed? But the moment had moved too fast for his senses, the croissant had distracted him. He did not know her. He was sure she did not know him.

But her smile left him swimming to breathe in a confusion. Someone else might have left his unfinished croissant and coffee and followed Miri. But Raphael was an expert in admiring his visions from afar.

But today, something unexpected occurred. His vision left behind a chaos of words attached to an explosion of emotions. Words were something else Raphael always had difficulty with. He felt a new sensation, happy to attach words to his feelings. Feelings with words were new to him.

Words would not break his heart.

The final pieces of croissant and sips of café con leche did not offer the needed comfort any more. Nor did it take away the ache in his left knee.

Having already decided to spend the night in the albergue in Puente la Reina and rest his swollen knee, Raphael was surprised he was re-evaluating the decision. His new chaos would not let him settle. He felt uncomfortable with the new explosion of words building inside him.

And when Raphael was unsettled, he needed to move, to walk. He would buy two walking sticks and test them, he decided, but only till the next albergue. He had never used walking sticks before.

As soon as Raphael approached the Royal bridge, he tried to remember the road from Puente la Reina to Cirauqui, he could not. The new sticks from a shop on the calle were already helping, the pain on the knee was less as he learnt how to lift and adjust his body weight while taking the strain on his arms. Only when his knees complained on the steepest of all hills, that endless hill — where did that come from? — did he remember the way. Doubt and regret grew halfway up the climb. He should have stopped in Puente la Reina. What foolishness, what crazy madness was he following?

There were plenty of trees to either side of the steep path. It was hot, so he chose the trees with the largest shade, and using his mochila as a large pillow, he lay down in the cool earth and stretched his legs. His knee immediately felt better and he closed his eyes.

In that moment, had someone asked him why he was walking the Camino, he would have instantly replied, "I am following an angel."

And of course, no one was there to ask.

14

The First Glance

'Raphael!'

Sara's happy voice lit Raphael's face with a welcome smile.

'My guidebook says nothing about this hill'. Sara was hot, sweating, and breathless but effortlessly cheerful. 'Come on. Let's walk together,' she encouraged. 'I need help getting up this hill,' she confessed. 'This climb has been going on forever!'

Sara and Raphael busily chatted and were surprised to keep up with one another on the incline. Raphael's knee had calmed during the rest and even he was surprised at their pace, aided by his new sticks, when they began passing a silent family. Reaching the top, Raphael and Sara did not stop but continued to a waiting empty bench next to a water fountain, and, as if that was not enough, the bench was surrounded by freshly mowed, tree-shaded grass. Both rushed to collapse on the grass, remove their boots and socks, and took it in turns to let the cold water from the fountain bless their steaming feet.

'Thanks for the company.' Sara was grateful to Raphael. 'Have you noticed that steep hills and distances pass much quicker when you are busy talking to someone?'

Raphael felt glad for Sara's company too.

'You look different,' is all Sara could manage before lying on her back with arms and legs outstretched on the fresh, cool grass.

Approaching Cirauqui with their growing shadows in the late afternoon, the view was nothing less than a picture postcard. An ancient town perched on a hill, crowned with the silhouette of a church and castle.

The path to the town, surrounded by vineyards, quickly took away the day's heat and hurdles. Even the albergue, opposite a church in a small plaza, was framed with red blooming flower baskets. All the pilgrims who approached could not help but smile broadly at the gift after the long Camino day.

The albergue was comfortable, the bed was comfortable; the homemade paella and salad evening meal had been perfect. No one was snoring. But even a perfect albergue does not bring a perfect sleep. Raphael could not sleep.

The vision in the *panadería* in Puente la Reina would not release him. The words that filled his mind during his vision were too many and swirling inside him, threatening to keep him awake all night. Finally surrendering, he unlocked his notes app on his phone and allowed the words to escape. He had never tried to write his feelings before and was surprised at the number of words and sentences. But even when he finished, when he could not feel any more words and his fingers and thumbs felt stiff with the typing, he remained restless. Her smile and the way her eyes had caught him continued to seize his mind and his body. His attention was only distracted by something uncomfortable, a small stone he thought, digging into his hip. At first the discomfort annoyed him for taking his attention away from his thoughts. His hands wrestled with the bedding to find the offending item but he could feel nothing under him or on the mattress under his sleeping bag. Reaching into his shorts pocket, he pulled out not a stone but a coin he had forgotten about. He remembered the coin had fallen from his trouser pocket while he was undressing in the shower. He had picked it up and slipped it into the nearest safe place, his bed shorts. A coin he now remembered picking up that morning on the Mountain of Forgiveness.

He had hoped to reach the mountaintop before the sunrise but he had woken too late and the light on the mountain had already arrived with a cold, biting, brutal wind, and with it, a low cloud crafted to obliterate the views. Most pilgrims stopped to take a photo or two of the sculptures but then marched quickly over the top of the mountain to shelter on the other side.

But Raphael had to stop at the top even if the wind was trying to lift him. Like the passing pilgrims, he too was captured by the life sized metal-black silhouettes, but he had to remain inside the noisy upheaval. He sat, unclipped his mochila at the stone monument, and watched the theatre on the mountain as the magical artwork appeared and disappeared through the cloudy mist while real pilgrims rushed by.

The play, the lighting, the sound of the rushing wind, and choreography of the live show delighted him.

But there was another reason to stop.

A prayer. A prayer to be left at the Mountain of Forgiveness.

Raphael had only met Amelia the week before. She could not walk the Camino but had always wanted to learn more and the bar waitress, knowing that Raphael, another regular, was leaving in a few days' time, decided to introduce them. Raphael and Amelia instantly became friends. Amelia was mesmerised by Raphael's vivid description of his previous Camino. After Amelia explained the recent loss of her husband and described her grief, she asked if Raphael would carry a prayer to the Camino for her. Raphael suggested she write two prayers, one for the Mountain of Forgiveness, the other for the Mountain of Burdens.

'One is near the beginning of the Camino and the other near the end,' he explained. Raphael also tried to describe the Mountain of Burdens. 'Pilgrims carry stones, usually from their home,' he continued. 'The stones represent their burdens, and are left at a metal cross on top of the mountain. It is a beautiful place with a silent and yet captivating, very moving energy. Every stone left at the cross has a story, a memory. Some stones have photos tied to them, and some even names written on them. But most of all, they contain the sorrow, tears, the grief, the memories and the hopes of those left behind.'

He did not need to see Amelia's tears to know she was hurting and was looking for a way to heal.

'I will carry your words,' Raphael said, comfortingly. 'And one day, when you walk the Camino, you will find the words there, waiting for you.'

On top of the Mountain of Forgiveness, Raphael scrolled his phone messages and found the first prayer Amelia had sent him the evening before. He had not read the prayer. In fact, he had been worried about reading it on the mountain. He knew how important the words were for Amelia, how personal they were to her, for her. After composing himself, bringing his mind to the present, he messaged Amelia. *'I am here, on the Mountain of Forgiveness.'*

Raphael switched on the voice message on his phone and recorded Amelia's prayer with his voice. Four lines, each line began with the words. 'Forgive me'.

Finishing, Raphael paused and closed the recording. A prayer of forgiveness. He checked the recording had worked, attached the message with a photo of the metal artwork, and pressed send.

Raphael gave thanks for Amelia's prayer. Without the prayer he might have moved on, but because of Amelia's words he sensed and filled himself with a new energy. As if the mountain were reaching for him, replying to him.

When Amelia lost her husband, he had been alone, she was not with him, she never said goodbye.

Leaving behind her words, her grief, her prayer on the Camino, Raphael was glad to be part of his new friend's healing.

Raphael had felt the special energy of the Camino the previous year, but this was different. He felt more than energy, he felt a mystery. Something wonderful is here, he knew. And Raphael had no idea what it was. 'I am glad to be here,' he seemed to reply to the mountain.

Just as Amelia's reply arrived, a tear, a big hug and gratitude, Sara reached the summit. They had met the previous day on the way out of Zubiri and had walked to Pamplona together. Raphael made to stand and join her, thinking that she would continue walking. The wind was increasing in sound and force. But Sara planned to stop.

As Raphael stood, a gap in the mist allowed the sun to dive through and catch a discarded coin. The bright glint screamed at Raphael.

Noticing his pause, Sara approached following his gaze. 'Pick it up,' she shouted over the howling wind. 'Lucky penny we say in Ireland.'

Raphael, having had the decision made for him, picked up the wet and muddy bronze coin, and after a cursory glance, dropped it into a pocket.

'We catch up later,' he called to Sara as she sat, and

Raphael set off.

In the bed in Cirauqui, Raphael used the light app on his phone to inspect the coin. Dried mud obstructed the face of one side, but the other side was surprisingly clean and announced the year it had been made, 1968. A Spanish coin celebrating its fiftieth year.

He would be seeing his grandma in about ten days. She might appreciate the coin, he thought.

Raphael's warmest feelings of his youth were the teen years spent with his grandma. She and her home had provided him with sanctuary and love, a calm at a time when there was little calm in his life. He always delighted at the huge array of flowers in the house, fresh and dried. Once completely dry, the flowers were carefully stored whole or sometimes slowly taken apart and transferred into bottles. Each bottle would be labelled before being placed precisely in the right position in a remarkable cupboard of earthy colours and textures and shapes, and shelves of different heights to accommodate every size of bottle — a cupboard he loved exploring and he was always intrigued with the bottle labels. He had never learnt braille and he used to touch the labels to see if he could read the patterns. But he never learnt to see without his eyes.

Adjusting his eyes to the light and inspecting the coin a little more, first he thought the pattern on the clean side was the imprint of a lotus flower. But as his eyes followed the miniature shape, he decided the pattern was not a flower at all. It was a geometrical pattern. He had seen it before. He remembered the pattern well. It was called the flower of life. A perfect gift for his grandma, he thought, putting the coin safely in his money pouch. Still unable to sleep, he remembered the torrent of words he had let fall into his notes app. He wondered how they would read so he opened the app again. The words carried him to the face that had haunted him all day. Beautiful, perfect, like a work of art, he thought. And although he had been too far away to see her eyes, he made himself believe that she was talking to his soul. Was it possible to fall in love so easily, he wondered?

Had Miri been present, she would have told Raphael that the beauty he saw, he felt, and had written, was inside of him, was a part of him. He was only seeing the beauty inside him, reflected in her. But Miri was not in the albergue at the time.

Unlike Miri, however, Raphael had never seen himself. Raphael had never seen his reflection in the mirror or indeed seen himself at all.

The only way Raphael could see himself was through the eyes of others.

15

The Face of Love

If a pilgrim had asked Miri why she left the *panadería* in Puente la Reina in such a rush, without finishing her long-awaited first café con leche of the day, she most certainly would not have confessed that she was running from the face of a beautiful angel. No one would have believed her anyway.

Miri was not ready for an angel. Any angel. Especially one with a beautiful face of love. Faces that she had convinced herself had been nothing more than fantasies, ghosts, childhood inventions, had never really existed. Faces that she had learnt to live without for so many years. Suddenly, now, the face in the *panadería* had filled her with a battle of uncertainty and the unlocking of hidden, buried memories, filled with fear. Fear that the angels had been real all this time.

Why now? In a *panadería* in Puente la Reina? During her Camino? She was supposed to be running from the memories of a broken heart, broken love, not finding new memories to run from.

The childhood Miri carried with her was surrounded by love. Exceptional in fact, and every time she remembered. But now, the face in the panadería had taken her to another memory, shrouded and veiled. She recognised the mask on the face, on the pilgrim, a mask that had hidden another life, another part of Miri. A part that brought dread to Miri.

That face in Puente la Reina was not welcome. Her café con leche in Puente la Reina was not welcome. The only gladness she felt was the taste of the freshly baked chocolate croissant which she had finished and the fresh air that greeted her escape.

Was the face real? And if it was, she could not bear to look at such a beautiful face of love again, and feel the agony of love again, and the pain of unfulfilled hope. Miri's memory touched the sharpness of the life of terror she had once lived. The terror of seeing love, other people's love.

But the angel's face was between her and the door.

She averted her eyes, made sure not to bump into anyone, trip over any chairs or tables, held her fear and rushed towards, and then put behind, the face from her past.

The horror of living, feeling, and sensing other people's thoughts and loves. A horror that demanded to be seen every time she opened her eyes. A demand that insisted she saw intentions and expectations of both the past and the future. Miri remembered the sensations, and the sensation made her sick. Physically sick. She had to stop by the side of the road to calm and drink some water. She was glad no one was around her to make a fuss.

She had not seen the person behind the face of the angel. She did not care to. Miri sped through the pedestrian street and followed the yellow arrows over the bridge, despite her protesting left knee.

Miri came to the Camino to be unseen. To be invisible. And most certainly not to see her past. Especially the face of an angel.

If the Camino was supposed to leave the past behind, what was the face doing here? Why was her past staring directly at her, here, on the Camino?

Like a storm, the face of the angel rained painful memories of childhood friends and family who held secrets she could see, and never share. Raindrops she had once wiped away. She remembered the drive home after the hospital conference on her eighteenth birthday. Tears of relief that now unleashed a cyclone.

How could she know she had also left herself behind?

Miri walked fast hoping to unleash a desperate dark shadow inside her that might erase the face of the angel. But the only shadows were in front of her. She was glad for her protesting left knee that would not carry her and her mochila past the next village. She was weeping with pain as she entered a little village, just before Cirauqui, and was relieved when she saw the sign for a coffee shop with an albergue and a courtyard. She dropped her mochila, surrendered to a waiting chair and closed her wet sobbing eyes hoping she would never have to open them ever again. The owner of the albergue had seen her limp to the chair. Seeing Miri so distressed, she collected an ice block from the freezer in the bar, wrapped it in a towel and, without a word, placed it in Miri's hand.

Miri sobbed even more on seeing the angel face in front of her.

16

The Call

As a child, Miri always wondered why everyone so easily ignored love, ignored the faces of love.

She watched lovers argue, loved ones hurt one another, and always waited for faces of angels to return at the moment of an embrace, at each moment of a smile, each act of love, each touch of love. Miri adored the faces which she understood, at a very young age, was love, and always smiled when the faces arrived.

But being the only one to see love is a lonely comfort. So when Miri felt lonely, she danced. Her not so ordinary dance did not need any music, and her dance was far from ordinary. Fresh paella, it was a celebration of the colours of love that she witnessed around her. Her dance was exceptional.

When Miri was eight, waking up after a night of snow that was quickly recorded as the highest snowfall in the history of the valley, Miri and her mother put on their winter coats, scarves and woolly boots and made their way to the market. Miri saw an irresistible, heavy, white carpet covering the entire town and blinking, shining ice crystals in the misty waking morning sun. Perfect for dancing, Miri thought. Miri pulled herself away from her mother's hand leaving her glove behind and began her dance. Miri danced around the ancient frozen fountain in the middle of the white plaza and around every market stall. The stall holders and market shoppers, wrapped in layers of winter clothes, watched the dance with astonishment and smiles until almost everyone in the plaza stood and laughed and watched and clapped as Miri came dancing through.

Resting on a cleaned and dry bench with her shopping, Mother followed Miri's dance and when Miri passed in front of her, Mother's eyes were drawn to her daughter's rhythmic footsteps trapped in the melting snow. Footprints that became faces of an angel before they melted away. Mother understood that Miri was still seeing angels.

Mother never stopped Miri from dancing, but always remained alert. With the passing years, Miri grew bolder and danced with the seasons, with the sunbeams, the moon rays, with the starlight, and she loved dancing the most when she was able to race with the wind. Sometimes the whole town would stop to watch Miri dance, as if remembering their own forgotten youth. But it was not their youth Miri's audience remembered, it was something they only had a recollection for, a feeling that had once been their whole life until they or someone decided for them that the only thing mattered in life was money and comfort. In front of them they saw a love so powerful, so true, so forgotten, that many had to turn their eyes away.

And not everyone realised the truth. Some became melancholy on seeing Miri dance, others were happy; a few even became angry. Angry that they had denied themselves love, or left their loves behind, or worse, allowed themselves to succumb to a belief that love that had to be locked away and hidden from the eyes of the world.

And Miri saw the emotions of love, the elation, the tragedy and the pain in each one of her audience.

One day, Miri did not dance. It was raining. Amma was shopping in the *pescadería*.

Miri waited on a wet bench outside the shop, her legs raised up to her chest and her head resting on her knees while holding a multicolored umbrella just large enough to cover her dreams. With a 16th century earthquake-damaged church facade and portico as the backdrop and an ancient *cruz* next to the bench, had someone taken a photograph it would have won an award, but there was no one with an iPhone nearby.

'Why are you not dancing?' her neighbour, the coin collector, who was carrying the morning's pan and leche, wondered loudly as he began to walk by.

'You're getting wet. Sit beside me and share my umbrella,' Miri demanded, repositioning the large umbrella.

The coin collector welcomed the gesture and complied, grateful to have a moment's grace from the rain even if the bench felt wet underneath him.

'I am watching the rain drops dance,' Miri replied

to the original question. 'Each drop of rain is dancing and I do not know which one to watch. It is like an enormous dancing class. A ballet. I think I now understand the word "choreography". I could never spell it before. Each dancing drop of rain is like a letter in the word, and all the raindrops together create a spectacular theatre. I am wondering, who the raindrops are dancing for? And why no one is looking at them?'

The coin collector did not reply. He was already inside Miri's words and was mesmerised by the bouncing and shattering dancing stories of each of the raindrops.

'But now I know why the earth, the wind, the trees, the insects and the birds have all stopped. They have all stopped to watch the dance of the rain. Like a celebration, a moment of prayer. So I have stopped to watch and pray too.'

The coin collector realised that, throughout his long life, he had never seen the dance of a rain drop landing on the ground before.

The coin collector's angel embraced Miri.

'I love how you lift my moments, Miri. The sky is grey, everyone is getting wet and annoyed and yet you see such light and beauty where others only see shadows and discomfort. I have never seen the rain dance before, and yet it seems familiar, as if forgotten by my mind and body during a forgotten time. I wonder what else I have forgotten about life and the world around me?'

Miri looked at the coin collector's angel face and

knew his eyes were wet, and not from the rain. Miri had already understood the love inside the face of his angel had a different power to the love that her mother and father had showered her with. Inside the angel of the coin collector, she saw melancholy, a memory of love. Lost love, lost moments of love. And she loved his angel because she saw that he loved her as he might have loved his own daughter. And when Miri began to see the melancholy that would soon take his life away, and be the last memory of his life, Miri refused to look.

And Miri, or her dance, was not always loved. The young man who owned the oldest bar in the corner of the plaza, frowned when Miri danced. As if waiting to frown. And some people are always waiting to be offended.

'She is dancing with the devil,' he would say from his shadow to anyone who would listen nearby. Ever since the shadow had taken him he was always waiting to see the devil.

Shadows do not hear the rhythm and music of the universe. And yet, when Miri danced, he could not help but stare. His shadow wondered at the innocence of her joy. His darkness remembered and touched a feeling deep inside him he knew he would never choose to possess.

Miri chose to stay far away from the shadows of the oldest bar in the corner of the plaza. No angels of love ever appeared there. And when she passed the bar she never heard any music, not even the rhythm of her hearts.

When Miri entered her teenage years and her body could no longer hide or make excuses for her mask from her friends, all her friends became suspicious of the cracks in her eyes and called her a witch, a word that soaked her in terror. And so Miri began resenting the faces of the angels. And soon, she came to hate the faces.

Every time she saw the angel faces, love, she wept. And she wept.

She stopped wanting to see.

She stopped wanting to know.

And like everyone else who denies love, she stopped looking for it, stopped feeling, stopped knowing.

She stopped hearing the rhythm of hearts, the music of the universe.

She just wanted to be the same as everyone else.

And it was not that she stopped seeing angels. Angels were always there when there was love, at home, in the streets, at the parties, and especially when she danced love. But just as she wanted to see fewer angel faces, more and more, she saw fewer and fewer.

Ironically, when she discovered boyfriends, and later, a feeling she sensed was love, Miri made sure to hide every remnant of angels that she had seen before. To the point that even she stopped believing that she had ever seen the face of love.

Miri learnt to hide her gift from herself.

Miri, also, stopped dancing.

Miri lost herself.

In Puente la Reina, the face of an angel had looked at her. With a clarity and a vigor that she could not hide from.

And then, like a waking nightmare, every pilgrim on the road to Cirauqui, whether behind, in front, or when a pilgrim passed her, their angel of love began appearing and looking at her.

Miri wept her pain when she saw them.

Her knee hurt even more when she wept.

And the sight of the faces of so many angels frightened her. Her fear was not the face of the angels. Her fear was a realisation that in her life, her adult life, she had denied, nay, forgotten love, and the realisation scared her, brought tears to her. Tears, not just the loss of her love, but a sacrifice. Had she stopped living? Stopped seeing love? Why? And what was this rhythm inside her heartache?

And the feeling of being reminded what the music of the universe sounded like scared her. Scared that she might hear the rhythm of her hearts. And in that rhythm, find herself.

The Burden Collector again heard her call.

Miri had called the Burden Collector twice in one day. Hari had arrived twice. And twice he could not approach.

What is this place? The Burden Collector wondered. And Hari had never wondered before.

17

The Meeting

As soon as Miri closed her eyes, the rhythm began.

Music.

Familiar music. The rhythm lifted Miri's body. Miri watched her body being carried away. She watched the tears of misery she had collected during the day — or was it weeks, months, years? — being left behind. Where was she being taken to? She remembered the little girls in the beautiful sculptures on the Mountain of Forgiveness. *Take me there,* she ordered her dream. But her dream had its own path, its own music. When her body began to sway, to move to the music, she began to remember. She recalled a childhood where the only sound she heard was her music and, when she danced, she danced love.

And if any new tears fell at all, it was because her eyes were full of joy. Her body was full of joy. Full of love. A love that she once saw everywhere, in everyone. How could she forget her dance, her music, her love?

And when she woke to an alarm and checked her iPhone, it was 4.44 a.m. Her alarm was set for five a.m. She looked around to see which pilgrim's alarm was ringing. The realisation that the music was still inside her made her smile, a smile that turned onto a laugh. And she laughed again, glad that she was alone in the albergue, imagining the pilgrim faces being woken by a laughing pilgrim.

Stepping outside the albergue, Miri breathed the morning's fresh innocence. 'I'm sorry.' She put her hand to her hearts, and then with the words, 'thank you,' she stepped into a new day on the Camino. Miri reached for her iPhone. Some words she wanted to remember. She checked her photo album and there it was.

"Welcome to today. Another day, another chance. Feel free to change." A Camino message.

Miri laughed once more. *Perfect*, she said to herself. How had she allowed her fears to consume her. How had she turned her back on her innocence, on the faces of love?

She read the message once more, and, when the phone battery died mid-sentence, realising she had forgotten to charge the phone in the night, she looked up at the moonless starlit night. She heard an answer and knew she would not need her phone today.

The only feelings in Miri's body were the thrill of the walk through the starlit darkness until her eyes were captivated by the street-lit magic of a fairy-tale shaped little town on a hill, topped by a castle, ahead of her.

Miri listened to her hearts. Hearts that spoke with the world. A long-forgotten sound and a long-forgotten conversation. Hearts that echoed the rhythm of her soul, hoping, one day, to meet the soul. And walking and waking into the starlight, she remembered the walk out of St Jean Pied de Port. But as much as she tried, she could no longer count the days since the climb on the Pyrenees. Days and nights had become one long movement.

She remembered her dream and she remembered the rhythms from her childhood. She remembered the love she had shared with her lover. The passion, the depth of a love that had come from deep within her, a love she had given away. What had he done with that love she wondered for a moment? The day he typed, 'Its over', on Facebook, it was important to her where it was typed; what happened to all the love she had gifted him?

Was there more love, as deep, inside her?

The streets of Cirauqui should have been silent, echoing only to Miri's footsteps and her music. *What is this music I am hearing?* Miri asked, looking at the stars. *Is this the music when heartbeats and souls meet under the stars?* The music was hypnotic; she wondered if she should dance through the cobbled, sodium-lit orange streets. She wondered if she would remember how to dance, even if she tried. Reaching the far side of the town and a path that led away from the magic, Miri asked the stars once more, 'Will my hearts know love again?'

The stars could not answer. If they could, the stars might have reminded Miri that it was not her hearts, but her soul that loves and sees the faces of angels.

And with so much of her before forgotten, Miri's

numb ears and cold nose suddenly remembered the morning cold. Her fingers felt almost frozen. Pulling her hat over her ears and wrapping a scarf around her neck, she realised the street lights had ended and the path ahead was descending into a dark mass of blindness. A few steps further and looking down, she was shocked not to be able to see the ground or her feet.

No torch to find the yellow arrows. Her phone battery was dead.

Raphael slowed.

At first he hesitated, pretending to appear as if he were adjusting his mochila. Walking the Camino under the starlit mornings had its problems. A dark and silent silhouette ahead, inside the before dawn darkness of an empty country lane, waiting in the middle of the path, was a good excuse to invite a little anxiety.

Reassuring himself the shape was a pilgrim and not a bandit, Raphael stepped forward, albeit a little slowly. He thought he would walk behind the apparition but quickly caught up as the pilgrim had stopped. He already understood why when he felt the uneven path under his feet and his eyes entered the pitch darkness.

One word.

'OK?' Too early for conversation, too dark for introductions.

'I cannot see the way.'

Raphael noticed her European accent first and only then realised she had no torch.

'I have walked this way before,' he assured the

voice. 'Stay close behind me and follow my torch, I will point it at my feet. We can walk slowly.'

And so Raphael's smartphone lit the way for himself and his new companion. He knew she was nervous. She was being led into and through the ruins of an unlit, ancient Roman bridge, in the dark, by a stranger. The obstacle course was strewn with big rocks and small stones, narrow paths, narrower steps led down, and finally a difficult to see rocky climb. There was relief when they inched their way out of the ruins and were back in the open. Soon they were on a well-lit modern flyover that crossed a highway. The Camino arrow at the end of the bridge confirmed the way.

No words needed.

Only when some early dawn light began to paint the new green of the day and nudged Raphael awake did he remember to offer an introduction.

'Raphael, from Italy.'

'Miri,' the well-wrapped scarfed figure replied.

Neither felt the need to seek the face of the other. It was still too dark to see anyway. Looking ahead was all that mattered. Feeling the companionship and kindness of a stranger, and hearing the assurance of each other's voice, the voice of a shared pilgrimage, was all that mattered.

Later, when Raphael remembered that morning, he would startle when describing the moment as one of the most beautiful and perfect he had experienced in his life. Two strangers meeting in starlit darkness. One leading the other into an unknown, walking and waking together through trust, human presence, with care and kindness. Neither knowing nor needing to know what the other looked like, who the other was, what shape they were, how old they were. Nothing mattered. Only each other's presence on the Camino.

The first coffee of the day mattered to Raphael.

'Another hour to the next village, to the next bar,' he estimated, already imagining the café con leche, the only reason for putting one foot in front of the other at this time of the morning. His companion might have been thinking the same but Raphael did not ask.

Raphael and Miri amazed when a small stretch of well-preserved and perfectly laid Roman road opened ahead like a scene from an ancient story. A Roman road waiting for a Roman traveller!

'Wow. I am stepping on history,' Raphael said, startled.

It almost felt wrong to walk on the expertly laid stones. But they were also wet after the night's rain, uneven, and the struggle for balance kept the two pilgrims occupied. Their walking sticks saved them both from injury and more.

Passing a campsite inside one of the olive groves, a sign even offered breakfast, gave some hope for an early hot drink, but no one was awake in the camp. Finally, in Lorca, a small albergue and bar was just beginning to wake when they arrived.

'Café con leche, freshly squeezed orange, and

croissant,' Raphael ordered first, smiling at the welcome warmth that had already begun to creep into his ears and nose as his face resumed his normal colour.

Miri too ordered, sat and spoke her gratitude. 'Thank you, for rescuing me.'

The first coffee of the morning on the Camino is always a gift and a treasure. Today's treasure was her knight, her saviour. The cold would soon be forgotten.

Raphael nodded. His companion was still camouflaged by a hat and scarf and all her morning layers.

'Today's morning trek to the first bar was short,' he offered. 'If I reach Villamayor tonight, it will be 12 km before the first coffee stop tomorrow morning.' Raphael laughed.

Miri was intrigued and decided to check her map as she began unwrapping her morning layers.

Raphael jolted when he recognised Miri's face.

So Miri was her name.

Miri looked up from her guidebook and smiled. She smiled at Raphael and smiled again at his angel.

When their eyes met and he captured her smile, Raphael tried not to look embarrassed. It was not the café con leche that warmed him this morning.

A surprise.

A morning without words.

A meeting that was already a memory.

A meeting under a starlit Camino.

18

The Flower

Miri was no longer scared of Raphael's angel.

As they walked on from Lorca, the pace quickened. Miri was surprised to find that she felt safe with the face of the angel next to her. A face that, Miri knew, adored her, but a face that did not know her.

'I remember a wine fountain in Estella.' Raphael was suddenly nervous with his new walking companion and felt the need to fill the silence.

Miri had read something about the fountain in her guide book but had not taken it seriously.

'Last year I arrived too late. The fountain was empty. I think they only fill it in the early mornings.'

Miri laughed. 'A wine fountain!' And as she laughed, Miri felt her body, mind and soul reconnect to a calming energy around her. She had not smiled or laughed in many days. Miri wondered about the Camino and the arrival of her companion just at the moment she needed help. She needed to learn to trust and read the universe better, she thought.

'That Roman road was incredible this morning. But I must remember to charge my phone.' Miri admitted her folly.

'Unless you know the way in the dark, it's better to walk with someone,' Raphael suggested. 'And in the dark, if you are with someone, it is quicker to find the yellow arrows when you are lost.' And then Raphael shared a few stories from his previous Camino. Walking in the mornings, following others with torches, being lost, and finding others lost. Miri felt better knowing that she was not the only one who had made a mistake. She would be better prepared next time.

Only the universe knew, there was no such thing as a mistake.

As Estella neared, Raphael slowed on the downhill sections to tend to his complaining left knee. Miri's knee was no longer hurting so she continued ahead.

The rush and rumble of the fast-flowing river was the first to call as Estella approached. Enjoying the fresh conversation with the gushing sound, Miri had a fleeting wonder if there was a safe place in the river to dip her hot sweaty feet. She looked towards the river and received the invitation.

As if placed especially for her, an empty bench was waiting for Miri to sit and remove her boots and socks. A wave of pleasure flowed through Miri as she placed her feet on the soft, cool, green carpet and she felt the touch of the living grass and earth rising to caress her feet. She walked towards her invitation. But as she stepped closer to the river, she understood the voice she had thought was inside her was not hers at all; was it the river that was calling? And then, as suddenly as her dream, she stepped into a moment that even surprised the Bull. And nothing had surprised the Bull before. The Bull had not known surprise, or a before.

Miri stepped towards a bright myriad of small yellow eyes amongst the fresh green wild grass and the grey purple of the wild puppy dog tails. The eyes beckoned her to come close and sit. Miri's eyes were already captured.

The voice inside grew louder. This was not a dream, she knew, but she could not say whether she was making the decisions or the flowers were deciding for her. Dropping her boots, socks and mochila first, Miri was enthralled to sit amongst the admiring eyes of the flowers.

If Miri sat and stared at the flowers, so did the flowers stare at Miri. Everything Miri was thinking, the flowers appeared to be thinking too.

'An echo,' Miri decided. 'I am listening to an echo, a voice in my mind. But I can sense you have a voice.'

Miri continued to stare at the yellow eyes. 'I have never seen flowers like this before.' Miri paused. 'Like you, before,' Miri corrected and decided to speak to the voice she had not yet heard.

'I have never seen a girl like you before.'

'The pink veins in your petals are like tiny pulses of life.'

'You have pink veins too. I have not seen a face like yours so close before. I can feel a rhythm inside your body, four rhythms. And there is music.'

Miri thought she was mad. She was speaking with a flower.

She wondered who the prisoner was. The flower, her mind, or her eyes.

'Like no other flower I have ever seen.'

'Few have seen me and not many see me. I do not belong here.'

She found the mutual stare and the conversation both bizarre and mesmerizing. She was in a daydream. Miri remembered the angel faces of her youth. Was she creating a new fantasy, a new imagination?

No. Miri breathed. She sensed, and felt a life in this voice, in the flowers. She wondered what consciousness lived inside this little explosion of colour in front of her.

'Those who have seen me, called me a secret.'

And if the flower was a secret, why was it talking with her?

'We will both live life today.'

Only two of the words stayed with Miri, the fourth and the sixth. In that moment Miri felt lives, her lives, she saw a history, she saw a sensation that she knew was her past, and then she sensed her future.

'How do you know?' Miri should not have been shocked, but she had to accept her new reality.

The voice of the flower ceased, at least the words stopped, but Miri continued to sense the flower and through her sensations, the conversations continued.

The flower connected with Miri. It was Miri's turn to invite the flower to enter. Miri introduced the flower to her past and the flower explored all the hearts she had ever seen. And then the flower saw the future of all the hearts inside her and explored her frozen hand.

The words that Miri understood, life, death, time and love, confused the flower. And when the flower explored the feelings contained in these words, the flower was confused even more. But Miri was not confused by the story that she was being shown, the request the flower was making.

The flower kept her stare, kept her body, kept her soul and rested itself inside Miri's frozen hand.

Unspoken thoughts.

The future of the flower was her future if Miri chose.

How long she had sat in meditation with the flower, Miri did not know.

When Raphael's shadow reached her, Miri felt a wave of electricity that made her hair stand on end and sped her to the present.

But even as she jolted, the flower spoke one more time.

'You will carry me.'

Miri had accepted the truth.

'Let me help you,' said Raphael, realising what Miri was about to do. He held open the book Miri had already removed from her mochila, the book she had been reading in the evenings, an ancient tale of a group of travelers at the time of Abraham.

'One flower,' Raphael heard Miri say, 'only this

125

one.'

Raphael watched Miri being guided to choose the waiting jewel.

Miri and Raphael did not speak through Estella and both appeared to limp a little more heavily on their way to and from the supermarket.

The wine fountain came soon after.

'That was the best wine!' Miri had to admit. She had assumed the worst.

They both celebrated the morning with a picnic of fresh bread, cheese, tomatoes, onions, olives and the sweetest cherries.

'And this is the best lunch. What a great idea. Someone seems to be looking after me today.' Miri let her thoughts escape into Raphael's angel.

'Everything tastes better on the Camino.' Raphael laughed. 'We are fortunate today,' Raphael agreed, not fully understanding. 'Last year I only met a few people who had tasted the wine. Everyone else said it was empty.'

They both laughed at their fortune.

Miri felt as if she had just woken after seven years.

That night, on her bunk bed in an albergue run by international volunteers in Villamayor de Monjardín, when Miri opened her novel to read, the albergue was filled with a beautiful scent. The night held the sweetest sleep and the sweetest dreams for all the pilgrims in the albergue.

In the morning, if the waking pilgrims had asked

each other, they would have shared dreams of angels, flowers, rhythms and music that came from the stars. But since the morning pilgrims observed the morning silence, the dreams were forgotten, replaced by yellow arrows to guide the way.

19

The Flower Collector

'Amongst the memories of our family, there is an ancient tale of a mustard-yellow orchid with pink veins that run through its petals, and its petals are shaped like the wings of an angel.' Raphael heard the story for the first time as a little boy while staying at his grandmother's house, and she would always end the day delighting Raphael with her bedtime stories.

'The tales say that in the centre of the orchid is the shape of a red heart, and if one stares at the heart long enough, the heart begins to beat.' Raphael never forgot the description of the flower.

'Few accounts of the flower remain. And while every account differs in almost every detail, on three points every account agrees. The first is that the flower only blooms on one particular day of the annual lunar cycle, and only during the alignments of five planets. The second is that the flower only grows in one tiny corner of the universe described as a small patch of grass near a river along an ancient pilgrimage in northern Spain. Most of us understand the pilgrimage to be the Camino. One of the accounts even claims that the flower is to be found along the river that passes a Roman road that leads to the Fortress of Lizarra.

'But how anyone can be sure of any of these stories has always been a mystery, Raphael. Since the final point, every account contains and agrees, is that the flower is only visible to those who have seen an angel.'

Raphael loved his grandmother. Loved her stories. She made time for him, doted on him, loved him. And her stories were always fantastic fantasies.

But when Raphael heard the story of the flower once more, this time in his teens, he already understood that the narration was not just a telling, but a recollection, a memory. Raphael wondered why Grandma Ava told the story as if her life depended on it.

'Why do you remember the story, Grandma?' Raphael felt old enough to ask. 'Why is it so important?'

Ava had a way, Raphael knew. She would reply, but only when Raphael was old enough to understand the reply. The reply arrived a year later. Raphael had come to live with his grandma to create a distance from his warring, separating, and soon to be divorcing parents.

'The memories I carry have been passed to me for many generations, Raphael, and begin with the exile of our family from this land. You understand the word exile?

Raphael nodded.

'Our family were driven from their land, their

129

homes, more than five hundred years ago. A period of religious venom.'

'Poison?' Raphael needed to check.

'A poison that filled the hearts of the world when eyes watched in silence as Jews and Musulmanes, anyone not of the Christian faith, were told to leave their homes. Dark days. Days to be remembered, Raphael. Persecution because of faith is vile. In fact, our temples still hold an annual prayer on the day of our exile.

'Our family in Spain were poor. They did not have enough possessions to sell. Some of their land and homes were bought at the lowest prices by traders who took advantage of our misfortune. Other land and homes they could not sell were abandoned. The family could not afford the greedy, inflated prices on the transport ships that would carry the exiles away from Spain. So our family joined the march with those who began their exile on foot. Their journey was full of danger, both bandits and people who wished them harm. Their path took them through the mountain passes across the Pyrenees, through France and into Italy. Winter halted their march in the shadow of the Dolomite mountains and they were forced to find shelter. Our family worked, traded, raised money, and when they had collected enough, in the spring of the following year, the family split. Some of the family chose to remain in Italy where they had been made welcome. They are your ancestors. The remaining members of the family continued the journey to the coast. And there, they booked passage on trading ships to the holy land.'

'But you are still in Spain,' Raphael remembered saying.

'About a hundred years after the expulsion, a small group of our now Italian family, intrigued by their Spanish roots, even with the knowledge that Spain was still a land of persecution, were determined to return and reclaim their ancestors' land and homes. They journeyed to Spain. I do not know if they were able to reclaim anything, but I do know they settled in Burguete. And amongst the family that settled in Burguete, was a young woman called Clara — her original name was Chiara, I believe. We know she returned to Spain for a very particular reason, not for land or property. She was in search of a special flower. The silent heart she called it. The secret flower. An orchid.

'She was very brave. To return to a dark land, a land with no heart, took courage. Clara of Burguete-Auritz is the first, in the memory passed down to me, of the line of flower collectors that I carry. Before Clara there was another line of flower collectors. But I only carry the line from Clara. Her haven was the forest around Roncesvalles. She collected the wild flowers that grew in the forest and from which she made remedies and elixirs. It was Clara's grandchild who, while collecting flowers from the forest of Roncesvalles, was captured by the zealots. She was taken, accused, imprisoned, tried for witchcraft, and burned.

'Once more, the world watched in silence as innocents were burned alive.

'It is said that her name, along with the names of others who were burned, is written in some corner of a plaza where the burnings occurred. But I have never seen any plaque of names.' Raphael's grandmother always laughed at her own jokes.

'Members of our family who witnessed the evil burning described men of their so-called god standing around our Clara, quoting from their religious texts, while she screamed in the flames. On that day, our family in Spain made a promise to one another that they would remain and always search for the flower their kin had died looking for.

'When news of the burning reached our family in the holy land, one of the elders who was now in Jerusalem added one more ancient memory. She recollected the stories she had been told as a child by Clara's mother. A foretelling, she said. The flower collectors should only remember, and not look for the flower.

'From her we learnt that our purpose was to wait and prepare for the arrival of the flower. That the flower will be brought to one of us, the flower collector, only when the right moment revealed itself. Of course, many of our young, in their zest, did look for the flower. And of course, not one managed to find it.

'The flower has a name, it is called the silent heart. It is the flower that will make the elixir for the silent heart.

'I am one of the line, Raphael. And the last. My ancestors each passed on the knowledge of the mystery of flowers and their elixirs to their children, and children's children. We know, have accepted, that one of our line will, one day, receive the flower and make the elixir. I must wait for the flower, Raphael. Since I am the last of the line, the flower will come to me when the time is right. And I must be ready to receive the flower, Raphael.'

'Why are you the last, Grandma?' Raphael remembered asking, even if he already knew the answer.

'I have no children, Raphael. This is why I trouble you with my stories.'

With all his grandparents having passed away before he was born, his great aunt had always been Grandma to Raphael, and would always continue to be so.

'What will the elixir do?' Raphael had wanted to know.

'That knowledge appears to have been lost through the ages of our storytelling, Raphael. I can only tell you what has been handed down to me. All I know is that the elixir will be a remedy the world has never seen before and will never see again.'

'Will it heal, Grandma?'

'I am not clear, Raphael. The elixir is not one that will heal the damage caused by disease, or war, or excess. It is not a remedy for age or illness or time. The orchid is called the silent heart. And the elixir will be a remedy for a silent heart. A remedy that will only speak to a silent heart.'

'What is a silent heart?' Raphael asked once more.

'I am glad you ask, Raphael. At least you are listening and I am not boring you. To me the idea of a silent heart has no meaning. But the flower collectors also believe that only after the elixir is made, the meaning and purpose will unfold.

'You are my great-nephew, Raphael. After everything I have told you, should you choose, you might try to look for the flower, but do not try, you will never find it.'

'I do not understand?' Raphael was confused.

'This flower is no ordinary flower, Raphael. It was left behind by an angel. An angel who once taught our ancients how be good kings. During a time when kings could speak with angels. The first ten kings of the world, Raphael.'

Raphael was still confused.

'Only those who have seen an angel can see the flower.'

The collector of flowers knew all the flowers. Not from their colour, but from their scent and their touch, their texture and their shape. And more importantly, their presence, their being. She knew that flowers have a power to be seen or unseen, to be known or unknown.

The Flower Collector knew she would never see the flower.

In fact, the Flower Collector had not seen anything for a very long time. The collector of flowers was blind.

20

Villamayor

After Villamayor de Monjardín, Miri and Raphael found themselves waking at the same time, walking at the same pace, taking the same breaks, even surprising themselves with their similar cravings for coffee, quiet, and conversation.

And each night, when Miri opened her novel, the words of the story gave her comfort and the flower's bright sunshine colour, its red veins and petals like angel wings that appeared to flutter, all remained perfectly preserved in the pages of the book. If the sight of the flower did not speak with her, the scent did, describing something still to be discovered.

Ever since Miri had picked the flower, the flower had offered no words. One night in Grañón, when Miri opened the book and the pages opened to the flower.

'I am walking to Santiago, where are you going?' Miri asked, almost expecting the flower to reply. But the flower gave no reply.

'The scent is getting stronger,' she said to Raphael.

As Burgos approached, Miri did not notice the scent of the flower any more. For the scent had become the scent of her dreams, a deep beautiful sleep that carried all those around her to the other world. A world of angels and butterflies.

And as Hari watched, Hari found Miri's dream. The light inside the dream captivated Hari. So he followed Miri inside.

Dreams are confusing.

For Hari, this moment was the same moment as collecting her Amma's burdens, for Hari had no experience of time.

Hari had entered many dreams.

Souls journey in dreams. Hari, sometimes, collected burdens from inside dreams. Dreams called nightmares.

But this dream did not have a burden, only a light. The light was familiar. When Hari entered, he knew the source of the light. The light was the mystery Miri held in the fist of her left hand.

The light that did not belong amongst the living. The light did not belong inside Miri's dream. But the light was the force Hari wanted, intended to possess.

Hari stepped deeper into Miri's dream expecting to touch the force, maybe even grasp it. But the dreamer was on the Camino, and the dream would not allow Hari to take anything.

Dreams are confusing. Hari was confused. Spirits should not be confused.

In Atapuerca, Miri was confused. She could feel the music inside her. Day by day, the rhythm was stronger, louder. If there was such a thing as a Camino energy, she wondered why she could not feel it. The thought confused until she climbed the hill and wondered upon the site of the magic she thought she had been looking for.

Miri screamed, dropped her mochila. 'It is an ancient maze,' she laughed rushing towards the stones. And for the first time on the Camino, she danced for love. For the angels of love. She danced through to the middle of the maze and then back out again. And she would have carried on dancing had Raphael not called, 'How do you hear the music that makes you dance?' Raphael had caught up and been watching.

Miri stopped. 'The music is stronger inside me now. It has always been there but I had forgotten how to listen. Now, when I stand still, it is as if I miss my own heart beats. This maze is what my body was waiting for. You have to dance into the middle to know how to dance out again. And only after you have danced out do you discover what you found in the middle.' Miri lifted her mochila, cradled it to her back and they began walking again. 'But there is one more reason I dance, Raphael,' Miri had not finished. 'The Camino is different to the rest of the world. I do not yet know how or why. But I do know that here, for the first time, maybe the first place in my life, I feel I can be myself, I am accepted for what I am. I do not think there is a Camino energy here. I think we bring our energy to the Camino. Here, I do not need to pretend and be what someone else wants me to be.'

'I understand,' nodded Raphael; he felt the same. 'No one cares if I am a man or a woman,' Raphael continued. 'How old I am, how I am dressed, what I look like in the morning and which country or religion my papers say I belong to, how many scars I have. Each morning we wake, tread the same path, walk in the same direction, but at our own pace. No one judges me when an 82-year-old walks faster than me, or when a blister makes me walk slower or if I stop to rest for a day because my knee hurts.'

Raphael's words touched Miri.

'I have a memory I have never shared with anyone, not even my parents. To do with this hand.' Miri lifted her frozen left hand. 'You know I cannot open my hand.'

Raphael waited.

'It was my 18th birthday. A friend, he was also our neighbour, was a coin collector and his gift for me was a small pink velvet bag containing a set of eighteen 1960s Spanish peseta coins.

'"The coins are very common. Of no value,"' he told me, wishing me a happy birthday. And he hoped that with the coins, I might start my own collection.'

'And did you?'

'No,' Miri laughed. 'Never had the time, but one day I might. Stop interrupting my story!'

This time they both laughed.

'I was thrilled to receive a selection of his coins. They came from his collection and I knew how important they were to him. I went to my father's study and found his magnifying glass. I returned and started inspecting the coins. Each coin had a different pattern on one side and I remember trying to identify the patterns when an itch began inside this hand. But the hand is frozen. You cannot scratch. Do you understand?' Miri lifted her hand again for effect.

Raphael understood.

'Painful,' he agreed.

'When I was very small, I used to insert all sorts of things inside to get rid of the itch,' Miri laughed at the memory. 'And my parents used to scream and shout. Once, I even tried to stick a fish knife into the hand.'

Raphael made a face. Trying not to laugh.

'Don't laugh, the itch was terrible. But on this day, my eighteenth birthday, the nearest object I had, and it was in my other hand, was the small coin I was looking at.

'I have no idea what possessed me, but the itch inside the middle of this palm was extreme. It did not wait for anything. I did not even realise how fast it happened. I began to force the coin into my palm to catch the itch through a small gap under my thumb and forefinger. Here, can you see?'

They both stopped walking so that Raphael could take a look.

'I know it is too small for coins, but the coin in my hand was small so I had to try to reach the itch. I was shocked when the force of reaching the itch forced the coin, completely, into the gap. It went all the way through.'

'No!' Raphael did not hold back his laughter.

'Yes! The coin disappeared. Into my fist.'

'What did you do?'

'I quickly returned the seventeen remaining coins into the pink velvet cloth bag and pretended that nothing had happened. My parents were still talking to the neighbour and did not notice. I think my face spoke the truth. I was never any good at pretending. Mother knew I had been up to no good. But I was eighteen, a teenager, and moody. Mother knew better than to ask.' Miri giggled.

'What about the itch?' Raphael was intrigued.

'Surprisingly, the itch was relieved. I have never had to worry about the itch since.'

That night, in the centre of the old town of Burgos, in the small 12-bed parochial Albergue Santiago y Santa Catalina, an albergue resting above a small church, Miri opened her novel to read the last chapter.

As usual, her eyes feasted on the flower first, before beginning to read. She had only just finished the last words of the novel when Miri thought she heard a familiar voice. The same voice she heard in Estella, by the river. She knew the voice came from the flower. Actually, Miri did not hear any words. There was no sound. Was it a whisper? And the reason Miri could not concentrate on the thoughts that were entering her mind was because, at that precise moment, an itch began in the palm of her left hand.

For the last seven years, since her eighteenth birthday, Miri had rarely had an itch that threw her. The coin inside would often do the trick for her.

But the new itch was extreme, the type of itch she used to have when she was little. Miri panicked. She reached into her bathroom bag hanging from the bed above and pulled out her always-ready itch reliever. Thank God she carried one. Habit.

The itch was quickly relieved. Miri began to relax again. But something felt unusual in Miri's palm. Something was missing. Miri felt around the palm with the stirring tool.

She made an unexpected discovery.

The coin was no longer inside the palm of her hand.

Miri smiled.

21

The Arrival

The Flower Collector was weary.

Tired by age.

Tired of the pain in her joints that she could no longer control with her oils and elixirs.

Tired of her invisible gate. A gate that every pilgrim walked past but never saw. A gate that collected the essence of every passing pilgrim but never shared the Flower Collector's regrets.

The Flower Collector was also waiting. And she was not tired of waiting.

And today, as she eased into the rocking chair on the porch for her afternoon meditation surrounded by afternoon snacks, she was touched by a new presence in the air. Ava closed her mind to the distractions around her and allowed the scent to enter her body. She breathed deeply and the essence journeyed her to her mother, and grandmother. The sensation that grew inside her did not have a description, and when she tried to look for the words, she was suddenly lost in the memories contained in the scent of the words.

When she woke from the trance, 'The flower is on its way,' she told her silent dog.

The dog, an elderly, slightly overweight, white Turkish dog Ava had rescued as a puppy from the weekend farmers' market, looked at Ava. Even though Ava could not see, she knew the dog was looking and agreeing with her.

Ava spoke to her dog. Ava allowed the dog to be a dog.

The dog allowed Ava to be complicated.

The language of senses without sight was one of many languages Ava had learnt. Her father was very protective but her mother refused to treat her as an invalid. She taught Ava the skill of flower collecting.

When she was a child, the name of every flower was only a sound for Ava, but with the touch of the flower, the sound translated into not one, but many words inside her, words she repeated. As she grew older, she began to recognise the texture and vibrations in each sound, and with every word that followed, she saw colours. The resonance of every word quickly became a feeling. And even the pause, or emptiness between each word, was another colour.

Every touch of any flower became an epic sensation, a poem. Even the sun that kissed her face each morning became a story, a gossiping tale that told where the sun had been, which flower and insect the sun had woken and what the sun had seen. She did not need clocks and apps to know the time or the rhythm of the weather, or the phase of the moon.

Ava spoke with the universe. With the language of

the universe.

Ava had lived a long life. A life full of pleasures and wonders wrapped with joy, happiness, laughter, sadness, tears, black rice seafood paella, sweet Spanish peaches, and hot *Padrón* peppers from Galicia. And all her life she had waited.

But she was not satisfied.

Somehow, and to many it might appear a strange knowing, the Flower Collector understood that the end of her life was close. But she also knew that before the end, and therefore soon, the secret flower, the flower she and the generations of flower collectors before her had been waiting for, would find her. And so she was not, yet, satisfied.

Sitting on the rocking chair on her porch, eating her pickled olives and home-made goat's cheese, listening to old songs she had once danced to, she talked to her dog, wondering who would take care of him after her passing.

'If our wait is almost at an end,' she told the listening dog, 'my sacrifice will be your patience.'

The scent that entered the house that night changed again. The scent greeted the flower collector in a dream where she saw butterflies and angels. She told her dog about the dream the next morning. The dog looked at her and knew what she meant, he had dreamt the same dream.

And later, the same day as the dream, when the shadows were growing longer although she had not yet heard the footsteps that carried the flower, she heard the flower.

'I am here!' the Flower Collector cried loudly.

The dog jumped at the call. Ava had never called before.

'I have been waiting for you!' she called again. All my life, she wanted to add.

22

Elixir

'I am here! I have been waiting for you!'

The call caught every pilgrim near and far, and for one moment all the pilgrims walking along the Meseta paused and turned towards an unseen voice. Many do not see the unseen. And the yellow and orange paint-peeling house, veiled behind an overgrowth of wild shrubs, was most certainly unseen.

With no more to be heard, and nothing particular to see, each pilgrim stepped away from the pause to continue their Camino until only Miri and Raphael remained. Searching the silence, Miri found herself standing in front of a rusted, flaking, metal gate. Miri was sure the source of the call lay behind the gate. She could see a house teasing her through a green blockade of untamed growth.

Sensing the mystery in Miri's gaze, Raphael chose not to interrupt. Raphael already knew his grandmother's call was not meant for him. When the dog arrived wagging his tail excitedly, all Raphael could do was open the gate to the garden of the calling and invite Miri to enter. In this theatre, he was only the audience.

As Miri advanced through the gate the dog acknowledged her with a quick sniff and deftly moved around Miri to find Raphael's warm smile and the attention she was looking for. Meanwhile, Miri continued through the overgrowth along a stone path and had to slow her step when an elderly, thin and frail-looking woman, sitting in a throne-like rocking chair that appeared a little too big for her small body, came into view. But Miri was hungry, and her attention was quickly captured by a kaleidoscope of multicolored snacks laid out neatly around the rocking chair. Miri's eyes lit as she instantly recognised the cheese, pickled olives, cut tomatoes and freshly sliced bread. Stepping closer, Miri's nose caught the roasted garlic while her feet carried her towards a plate piled high with her favourite *pimientos de Padrón*. As she turned towards the woman in the rocking chair with the intention to introduce herself, Miri saw a sight that only a few weeks ago would have caused her panic, distress, even to scream and to flee.

Miri's heartbeats responded in kind. They began to race. Miri had to close her eyes, calm, and open them again. This was not a dream. Reassuring herself that the moment was real, Miri knew that this moment that had been foretold, long ago, by a universe she would never understand. Here, on the Camino? Why here? Miri would remember asking herself when recollecting the moment again. A moment waiting for Miri, or maybe a moment Miri had been waiting for. And so she stepped into the vision.

In front of Miri was no longer a frail old woman, but a woman exuding more magic and more love that she had seen in any other person. A woman with two smiling angel faces. And both were looking at Miri. Twice the love, Miri already knew.

Slightly anxious now, and like each step on the first days of the Camino, Miri knew she was entering a deeper, more intimate connection with another world. Not an unfamiliar world, but a world she had once rejected.

Raphael, a few steps behind Miri, was surprised at the confidence and control with which Miri unclipped and let her mochila fall to the side of the footpath in mid step. He watched Miri climb the two steps to the porch and sit, uninvited, on a waiting chair next to his grandmother. And then, rather cheekily Raphael thought, Miri began to help herself to the *pimientos de Padrón*, cheese and the olives.

'Mmm…' came the satisfied sound from Miri.

All the necessary words were already on the old woman's angel faces and the moment spoke with its own voice. The silent words had already invited Miri, welcomed her, reassured her.

Raphael looked, raised his eyebrows, but did not seem surprised at the two of them, or their silence. Instead, he picked up Miri's mochila and carried it to the porch. His grandmother and Miri did not take their eyes off each other. Raphael had never seen his grandmother behave in such a way with a stranger, or in fact, with anyone before.

Dropping his mochila next to Miri's, and enjoying the weightlessness with a muscle stretch, Raphael approached his grandma, kissing her on both cheeks.

'The winds told me you would arrive yesterday, but I was mistaken,' the Flower Collector replied sharply, still looking at Miri.

'You could not possibly know that I was due to arrive at all, Grandma. I did not tell you I was coming. I decided to surprise you.'

Miri said nothing. Words were not important when faces of angels were present.

Raphael, realising that his intervention was an interference, surrendered by settling on the porch steps next to the already settled dog, there were only two chairs and both were taken. He proceeded to untie and remove his boots, releasing his sweaty socks and relieved hot feet. Seeing Raphael, Miri was reminded to do the same.

The Flower Collector's words were waiting for bare feet. When her words began, it was as if the Flower Collector had been waiting all her life to tell her story.

She described her life as a blind woman in the village. How Raphael and his parents used to visit every summer after Raphael was born. She had no children of her own and being his only living great-aunt, and with no other grandparent, Raphael always called her Grandma and his parents treated her as a mother. When his parents separated, Raphael was fourteen. Raphael did not want to remain in a house full of anger and regret. He felt the unspoken screams. He came to live with his grandma.

Listening to the memories, Raphael remembered his childhood but wondered why Grandma was telling her story, and his, to Miri, a stranger she had only just met. He surprised himself at the revelation that he had never seen his grandma speak about herself to anyone before.

Ava described her mother, how she had passed down her knowledge to Ava. And Ava briefly described finding love, a love that her mother and father disapproved of but still led to a marriage.

'This was my parents' home. I began my married life in a small house in Burguete. When my parents died, my husband and I moved here. I learnt my art in this house from my mother, and everything I needed to collect flowers and make my elixirs was already here.

'My husband died not long after we moved from an illness I could not heal. No one can heal the heart.'

When Ava began describing her skill at making elixirs from the oils of flowers and how she collected the tears of the night, every morning, from the freshly waking flowers, Raphael felt a little guilty. He sensed, in his grandmother's telling, that she had been disappointed by his teenage lack of interest in her "hobby". With a pang of shame, he listened.

And then Ava told the story of the last elixir that

she would ever make. An elixir that would be made from a special flower that grew upon the footsteps of the first angels that stepped on the earth. That when the time was right, the flower, that only grew by a river somewhere between Cirauqui and Estella she believed, a flower that only a special person would see and would have special permission to carry, would arrive at her door and present itself.

The plates were bare and the shadows were long by the time the stories for the day were finished. The summer light would soon give way to the moonlight. Miri had still not uttered a word.

'You see them, don't you?' Ava's question was a statement.

Miri woke from the listening.

Raphael looked at his grandmother a little uncertainly. What was she referring to?

Miri nodded.

Miri already knew the old woman had seen her reply because Ava's angels smiled. But the smiles caused tears to flow and Miri wept. An inconsolable flood. The third and last time she would weep so deeply.

All her young life Miri had seen faces of angels.

Miri's mother had always warned her that seeing the faces would bring disaster to her, her family, and would ruin her life. The faces had destroyed and shredded every one of her relationships. Mother's words had come true. Miri had abandoned angels many years ago. Miri believed, was certain, the angels had stopped her from living, from experiencing love.

But what Miri was seeing in front of her made her question her decisions. In Ava, Miri saw a blind woman who was not blind at all. Ava saw the world through her two angels. And if the angels were faces of love, what beautiful world of love was the blind woman seeing? Experiencing? Living?

Miri wanted to see the world though Ava's eyes, through the faces of Ava's angels.

Miri asked herself, for the first time, if she had angels. She had never seen her own angels. She had not even sensed their presence.

Ava's world, Ava's sight, was a world she had rejected. Turned away from. Suddenly, now, she wanted to see. She wanted to see her angel. She wanted to see her world anew through the face of her angel.

And so she wept her regret.

Ava allowed the regret to flow. When Miri calmed, Ava consoled Miri.

'I have regrets too. Too many. I remember them every time I touch the gate to my house. That gate remembers everything, and yet it still opens every day.

'Embrace who you are, little one. Embrace your choices. Embrace your mistakes. Everything is you. Even your mistakes and choices, all of them, all you. Beautiful you. Embrace your being. There is nothing to regret. Because every decision and every mistake gave rise to a feeling and a consequence. And these consequences have brought you here, as it was always meant to.'

'My name is Miri.' Miri's broken voice finally arrived with gratitude while her hand picked a tissue from a fresh pack Raphael put on her lap and she wiped her wet face.

'Sweet name, Miri,' Ava replied. 'Call me Ava. Our meeting was arranged a long time ago. During the time of the first kings who spoke with angels.

'The flower you bring can only be seen by those who see angels. Now I understand. The flower was waiting for you.' Ava paused. 'So you are the flower bearer I have been waiting for.'

Miri could not help but stare at Ava's angel faces. There was no anticipation in the faces. There was a deep comfort. Love of course, much love. But there was also an emptiness, a space. Within the void she saw a reflection and she might have recognised a reflection of herself, but Miri had never seen her own angels. Miri was overflowing with questions, and answers.

But it was Raphael who spoke.

'Grandma, I know nothing of the angels you speak off. But I remember your bedtime stories. I know the story says the flower can only be seen by those who see angels. But, Grandma, *I* see the flower. I saw the flowers when Miri was collecting one and pressed it in her book. I hear it too.'

23

Whispers

It was Ava's turn to withdraw into her thoughts.

The sun had already withdrawn.

The universe is complicated, Ava thought.

'I have been waiting for this moment all my life. You have only just arrived. I had no idea how I would introduce myself, and yet I have already made my first mistake.' Ava appeared to laugh but Raphael thought she was also upset with herself. Raphael thought he saw a tear. He always knew when his grandma was frustrated.

'I made myself believe that I did not have any expectations of this moment. I prepared the way my mother and our ancestors had shown us. All my life I have prepared. And yet, here I am, surprised! And yet, also relieved the moment is here. To live the moment instead of waiting for it is a blessing. What will we do with this moment? How will it pass? What will happen this night? What would my ancestors say!' Ava's tear turned into a deep laugh that told a story of a sorrow that was a surprise even to Ava. Only Miri understood the sorrow.

A moment ago, Raphael had been happy to have

brought Miri to Ava. Raphael felt regret for his words, he was not part of this moment, this drama. This belonged to his grandma and Miri; he did not need to say anything. But before Raphael could offer his apologies, he saw Ava comfort him with a smile.

'Tell us.' Ava asked Raphael to describe his connection to the flower.

Raphael rarely spoke intimately with his grandmother. His grandma always knew more about him than he ever did, he thought. He had never felt able to put words to his feelings. But Ava's story, and now her request, drew his feelings and memories to a difficult time in his life. He recollected how seeing Miri's eyes the first time had drawn his feelings into words. He felt the same weight inside his stomach. He allowed the words to escape.

'I remember the first time I came to live with you, Grandma,' Raphael tried, wondering what words would arrive next. 'I was a messed up, confused teenager. You hugged me, and I remember returning the hug. I remember just holding on to you, not wanting to let go of you. You were the only feeling of warmth and comfort I had when I came to you. I wanted to feel your closeness, your love, that love was for me. Only me. And just holding on to you was the most important moment in my life, Grandma.' Raphael had never told his grandma this. But he knew she already knew.

'When I arrived, my head could not understand why my parents were not talking with me, not explaining what was happening and were arguing between themselves all the time, all day and all night. I was invisible. Invisible to them. I would walk through the room they were in and I felt like a ghost, like I did not even exist. You, Grandma, brought a calm and comfort at a time I desperately wanted to make sense of the world and what was happening around me. The love you gave was a surprise, unexpected, I had never felt anything as close as that before. Through you, I confess, I felt a mother's love for the first time.

'I know nothing about heartbreaks and nothing about what it means to fall in love.' Raphael smiled. 'I am still struggling with knowing myself. Knowing if I can love another. If I know how.' Raphael paused. He wanted to say he could not see himself. Instead, 'I am just learning to hear and feel my own heart. I do not know if I am ready to hear another's heart,' he tried, unsuccessfully, he thought.

'But then.' Raphael found a new set of words. 'On the Camino last year, I felt and captured a sensation that took hold of me. A deep feeling, it was inside me and yet all around me too. A feeling that gripped me closer and tighter every day of the Camino. This feeling I carried with me when I left the Camino last year, remained trapped inside. Not the whole feeling, just a yearning to feel it again. It would not let me go and has brought me back to the Camino this year. In St Jean Pied de Port, the feeling returned. I only sense it here, only on the Camino.' Raphael was finding the words difficult. He had not described everything he had intended.

Ava understood. 'Tell me about the feeling,' she said, smiling and encouraging him.

'It is always hard to describe the Camino. It is different to the hug you gave me. But, in some ways it is similar. When it arrives, it is sudden, comforting, and contains a surprise. The Camino holds me just like you held me. I had not understood what I was looking for, what my soul needed before the Camino. When I felt your hug I felt loved for the first time, and when I felt the Camino's embrace last year, I saw, for the first time, the sensations inside me when I saw the sunrise, the sky, the light, the trees and the moon. I felt touched by everything around me, as if I was experiencing my life for the first time.

'As I walked further along the Camino, memories, hurt and hopes emerged, long lost and buried parcels of deeply buried emotion I did not wish to feel at the time. I already knew what the parcels contained. And without the fear I carry when I am not on the Camino, I allowed the Camino to lead me to each emotion. The arrows were more than arrows. I slowly sensed the layers of pain in my body open like wounds. Every day I explore the fear and shake these emotions away, one parcel at a time. In the last few weeks, I am not sure what I am feeling, but I think I began to sense what you might call, me. The soul I chose not to touch or see because of my pain and scars.

'But there is much more inside these feelings, Grandma. There is a sound inside the rhythm of walking the Camino. I knew, when the moment arrived, and it has arrived, that I would speak of it with you.

'To begin with, the sound was only a sensation, a beat, a feeling. When I walked through the Meseta, after I visited you last year, I realised I was hearing not a beat, or a tune or a rhythm at all, I was hearing a whisper. What I was feeling inside me was a vibration inside the whisper. And the vibration was everywhere on the Camino. By the time I reached Santiago, the whisper was inside me, inside my skin, and even in my eyes. I did not understand all this while I was on the Camino, only afterwards when I returned home to Milano. I was no longer on the Camino but my body was still here, walking the Camino. When I was walking to work, walking home, evenings, weekends, during the silences when all I could hear were my footsteps, the quiet whisper was always there. At times I thought the vibration contained a word, words. But the words had no meaning. But I also knew the whisper came from a voice. I did not know that I had carried a voice from the Camino. It stayed inside me all year and continued to call me.

'People ask me why I returned to the Camino and few will understand. I had to return to the Camino and find the voice again.' Raphael felt more satisfied with this explanation but he had not finished.

'And then, on this Camino, many extraordinary

things happened. First I met Miri, and we began walking together. And then when you were picking the flower, Miri, I heard you speaking to the flower. I heard the flower reply. I knew immediately the flower was talking to you. I also knew it was talking with you. Of course I know flowers cannot talk. I was embarrassed to tell you that I heard the flower.

'Every evening when you opened the book containing the flower, the flower whispered to the night, to the stars.' Raphael paused and looked at his grandma.

In fact, Miri look at Raphael, wide-eyed. She had been waiting to hear from the flower each night! She only heard the flower in Burgos.

'I recognised the whispers, Grandma. I had heard the sound of them once before. I heard them in this house. When I would help you make the flower elixirs, do you remember? You tried to teach me and, yes, I know, I admit, I was a terrible apprentice.' Raphael laughed.

Ava was intrigued.

'Whenever we made a flower elixir, when you let me help you collect flowers and I began to help you extract the oils, I remember the colours. And the more elixirs we made, the colours became sounds. The sounds were the whispers, Grandma. The same. Whispers with no words, but they took hold of me and I would lose myself in them. You would tease me and get annoyed with me when I was not paying attention and I had to ask you to repeat instructions to me many times. I know you got fed up of having to repeat yourself, but the whispers kept distracting me and I also tried to ignore the whispers. To be honest, I did not know, I did not understand or accept where the whispers were coming from. I was so preoccupied with my teenage problems, my parents, I thought they were just sounds coming from the mess in my head.' Raphael laughed.

Ava laughed too. 'You were a mess, Raphael,' she agreed. 'You saw the flower and heard it speak with Miri?' Ava wanted Raphael to confirm it. 'I did not know you could see angels.'

'I cannot see angels, Grandma. When you and Miri talk about angels, I do not know what you are talking about. When I look inside myself, I see and feel nothing. But I can see the flower. I heard the flower speak with Miri. Do you talk to flowers? Do Flower Collectors talk to flowers?'

Ava raised her eyebrows and fell silent. This was not the foretelling she had imagined, even if she had imagined one.

Miri and Raphael's eyes met amid an expanse of questions. Miri understood. Theirs was not just a chance meeting along a Camino during a starlit darkness outside of Cirauqui.

'You were fourteen,' Ava said, rousing herself again. 'You wept that day you came with your little suitcase. You wept for a whole week,' Ava remembered. 'Every morning I would wake you and you would weep in my arms and every night you would weep on your pillow. I embraced you with all my love.

'You have always been scared of love because of the indifference you witnessed between your mother and father. That was not love, Raphael. You have nothing to do with the love your parents may or may not have felt for each other. Do not try to learn their love, Raphael, love is an experience. Your mother and father loved you. But to hide from their unhappiness, their disappointments, their marriage, they immersed themselves in their careers. By looking at the past to hide from the problems, they could not see that the beautiful child they created needed their love in the present.

'I loved you, my dear, like a mother, because I tried to fill the space of empty love your parents left. But I was selfish too. You filled the void of my not having my own children. I loved and love you as my own. I had hoped you would find your way to love, to a lover, when you left this house, to feel a deeper love your soul needs and is waiting for. But that love will only arrive when you are ready to receive love, sweetheart. Be patient.

'I had no idea, when you were helping me, that the flowers were speaking to you, that you were listening, your angel never gave me any clue. We never talked of flowers. I never asked because I never thought you were interested. I tried with my stories. I made them as entertaining as I could.

'I should have asked, listened to you. You hid yourself and your gift very well. Your hurt was opaque, and I could not see through the hurt you were hiding behind. Or maybe I was not looking deep enough.

'I have never seen myself. And I recognised your anguish as soon as you were born. I always knew, Raphael.'

Raphael could not see himself.

He could only see himself through other people.

He was glad his grandmother knew. Grandmothers always seem to know.

'It seems the Camino is removing the layers of past buried pain from your body, Raphael.' Ava said, comforting him. 'I am so glad you heard the call of the Camino and found Miri.

'Can you believe, the Camino is my doorstep and I have never walked to Santiago. Just as you do not know what Miri and I are talking about when we talk about angels, I do not know what you are talking about when you mention the Camino. You will have to tell me more.

'I hope you felt my presence, even if I did not always feel yours, and knew that my love was always here for you.

'I admit, I had only one expectation today, the flower. That means I had an expectation.

'You are teaching me, Raphael and Miri, that I did not learn the lessons of the flower collectors that came before me. But there is still time for me to remedy my errors.

'You have brought the flower, and the flower has brought us together. This flower, and the purpose of the elixir, may be no more than the simplicity or complexity of this meeting.' Ava paused. 'To answer your question, Raphael,' and Ava did not hide herself or her small ping of jealousy as she spoke. 'I do not hear the flowers, Raphael.'

Raphael was confused, maybe a little shocked. 'But you are a flower collector!' he protested.

'Their scent, and the vibrations of their colours in the light when the light reaches me, that is what I hear. And if you sense the same, I do not hear words, or a voice. You are describing a gift much more powerful than mine.' Ava spoke softly, almost blaming herself. 'I never looked into your heart. You and Miri are describing and hearing something spectacular. Miri can speak to flowers. Miri and the Camino are your teachers, Raphael; keep Miri close. Let the Camino guide you.

'You are both here, the flower is here. The day is almost complete. Settle into your rooms. I need to rest. There is food in the kitchen, help yourselves. Raphael will show you the house, Miri. Your rooms are ready.'

'How did you know to prepare both rooms?' Raphael had not even told her he was coming. How did she know he would bring a companion?

'You still do not know my craft, Raphael. Tomorrow, I will share with you all my knowledge of the flower and the elixir. Be patient and forgive me.'

Ava giggled at the events unfolding around her. She stood and launched into her evening routine of clearing the plates and tidying up the kitchen.

'Nothing like any of the foretellings,' she muttered to the dog a few times, smiling to herself.

'I should have known the meeting with the flower would not be easy.' Ava was ready to retire to her bedroom. Raphael had just finished his shower and Miri was waiting to enter. 'My family, my line of flower collectors, we have been waiting generations. I expected the arrival of the flower to overwhelm me. But it is not the flower that is the surprise, it is the two of you.' Ava gave a broad grin.

Miri had so many questions. And Ava had not even asked for the flower.

'I know, Miri,' Ava replied.

Miri had not said anything.

'There is still much to say and plenty to do. But now it is late. Let me use the bathroom before you shower, Miri. And once you have washed, eaten and settled, Miri, come and visit me in my room.'

'Ava?' Miri tried to argue. 'You are tired.'

'You have never met them, have you? I want to introduce you to your angels.'

24

The Oath

Hari found himself standing within the moment, on the Mountain of Oaths, where spirits took their oaths to obey, to serve, to protect and guide humans. Hari watched as the spirits, one by one, took the oath, were given their purpose and sent to serve those who were experiencing life, and love.

Hari had returned to the moment of taking his own oath. A moment at the beginning of time. A time during the reign of the first ten kings. And Hari watched.

But he was not watching any more, he was standing inside his spirit. A spirit ready to serve. He was in the now, in the present.

And as Hari descended from the seventh realm, as his spirit felt the presence of the earth, he found himself listening to the sounds of dissent. Sounds he had been deaf to before.

'Do not take the oath,' the voices said to those who would listen. 'They are beings of clay. Spirits do not bow to clay.'

And Hari stepped away from the oath.

Hari did not take the oath.

Hari had changed a moment. The moment of the

taking of his oath.

Hari had never changed anything before.

And if Hari had been connected to the universe before, to the light and dark, as he stepped away from the oath, he found himself attached to an unfamiliar darkness. A space inside a new unknown.

The Camino was unknown to Hari. Love was unknown to Hari.

And now, without the oath, Hari was free to destroy love.

Life was unknown to Hari. If by destroying love, life no longer had a purpose, Hari would be satisfied.

Time.

Hari was not supposed to understand time.

Something had changed.

Hari had changed time.

25

Dreams

When Miri crawled into her bed, her immediate intention was to wake early and continue her camino. The flower was where it needed to be. She had just been introduced to her angels. She felt submerged and wanted to explore the new gift that Ava had unleashed inside her. The world, the stars, even the night around her was not the same any more. She needed to walk alone.

And yet there were too many questions which, Miri knew, only Ava could answer. And leaving Raphael behind would not be easy, she already knew.

Finding herself embraced by fresh clean sheets and a soft down pillow and a quilt she had to hug close as it reminded her of home and her own bed, thoughts of waking and walking quickly escaped and Miri, for the first time on the camino, chose not to set her alarm. She read the final pages of her novel again, she found them moving and then she turned to the new emotions she was sensing inside her. And then Miri slept a dream from her childhood and even a bull with four horns.

Raphael dreamt just as he had every night since Miri had collected the flower.

Ava dreamt too. Ava dreamt of angels and butterflies. And Ava had only ever seen angels and butterflies after she became blind.

26

Morning

The cotton linen, soft and comforting her skin instead of the usual earnest sleeping bag, confused Miri as she opened her eyes. Was she still in the dream? Had the evening been a dream? Did Ava exist? The caress of the pillow which brought a smile on her face convinced her. There really was one other person in the world who could see angels. And then a question began pressing her, repeating inside her: what brought me here? What mystery is guiding me?

'I have been waiting for you for a very long time,' the flower replied.

'Too early!' Raphael complained loudly, throwing his head under his pillow in the next room.

Ava woke with a start. A shiver rippled through her body and the sweat of fear covered her skin. A dream, she understood. But dream memories, sometimes, during the waking, disappear with the dreams. And while Ava remembered the sensations, she could not remember the cause of the fear in the night.

The dream had arrived with the flower. The fear was in the dream. The cause of the fear was important. Ava had to find the fear again. And so Ava immediately attempted to retrace the night's journey. Ava continued the meditation as she washed, dressed, and collected the day's bread delivery from the gate where she paused a while to breathe the essence of yesterday's pilgrims. Making her way to the kitchen through the avenue of flowers that greeted their morning welcome, Ava greeted them in return as the dream pieces began to reassemble and the shadow that had woken her took shape. The dream was not in any foretelling either, she complained to her ancestors.

Ava hesitated before stepping into the kitchen. The shadow was powerful, a force she had never known before, felt before. Why had such a fantastic force entered the dream? A dream in which it did not belong? No answer arrived.

Entering the kitchen, Ava glanced towards the kitchen table and saw Miri and Raphael's angels waking with their silent coffee. In between them, Ava sensed, lay the flower, resting between the pages of a book.

Placing the bread on the waiting cutting board, Ava picked up the knife and began to slice the bread, still looking towards the flower.

The scent of the flower teased her through the aroma of the fresh bread. If the flower smiled at Ava by way of an introduction, Ava did too. Ava was moved by the greeting. Ava had not rehearsed or expected any greeting with the flower.

'Welcome to my home,' she replied.

Raphael and Miri both turned to look at Ava,

nodded and smiled.

Still too many expectations I have, she told herself and the flower. And Ava was glad to be hiding her emotion behind the basket of freshly sliced bread that she carried to the breakfast table. Raphael was ready with a pot of coffee and another filled with hot milk.

Miri blushed as Ava settled next to her. When Ava glanced towards Raphael's angel, she understood why.

With the aroma of fresh coffee filling her cup, to her surprise, a new essence reached Ava. Ava smiled as if in reply. The dream was not mine, Ava understood. Ava felt relief and a foreboding.

'The flower is filling the room.' Raphael was surprised that words had escaped his lips before the completion of his first coffee.

'You came to my dream,' Miri accused Ava. Miri decided to play with her new friend.

Raphael stared at Miri with surprised eyes. Miri had only met his grandmother the day before! He knew not to get involved. He was still on his first coffee.

'It was not your dream,' Ava replied, equally curtly. And then more gently. 'I cannot say if I was following, watching, if I was invited and led, or if I was actually dreaming last night,' Ava confessed.

Miri and Raphael looked at each other with knowing smiles. They had had the same conversation after their first dream together in Villamajor.

'Angels and butterflies?' Miri checked. She sipped her café con leche and tried to remember Ava in the dream.

Ava nodded.

'The dreams began the night after Miri picked the flower,' Raphael explained, still needing a second coffee to collect his words.

'Raphael never remembers the dreams. But I describe and explore new parts of the dream with him every morning, after our breakfast.'

'I remember only Miri, nothing else.' Raphael corrected. 'And you were in the dream last night too, Grandma? Did you see us?' Raphael was enjoying the Camino rest day, and not at all surprised if Ava had joined the dream.

Ava nodded. 'I saw both of you, I am still trying to remember more. You always make the perfect café con leche, Raphael, I have missed you.' Ava sipped her coffee like a prayer.

Raphael could not resist. Leaving his breakfast for a moment, he made his way around the table and hugged his grandma. 'I have missed you too, Grandma. Buenos días.'

'Every night, you say?' Ava asked when Raphael released her.

Miri and Raphael both nodded.

'There is much to share today. Let us begin with the dream.'

'Can we finish our breakfast first?' complained Raphael.

'No,' Ava was impatient but paused to enjoy her

coffee.

'The dream is not yours. The dream belongs to the flower.'

Miri and Raphael did not appear surprised but the revelation silenced them both into a reflection.

'It is not you who has been exploring, Miri, the flower has been learning about you, from you. Listening to your hearts. Since you are both in the dream, you are both important to the flower.' Ava enjoyed the coffee once more. 'You have been living your lives again, each night, in the dreams. The flower has been experiencing life through the two of you. The scent in this house is full of life, many lives in fact. And not only the flower's. The scent carries the touch of everything the flower has experienced in the dreams. I even sense the movement and the changing life along the Camino,' Ava laughed. 'Imagine, the flower has walked the Camino and I, the Flower Collector, have not.'

'The dream is the flower?' Miri checked and nodded with amazement.

'The dream was always the flower,' Ava confirmed. 'And now I too have been in the dream, and the scent of the flower carries me, and my lives too.'

'The flower is listening even now, Grandma, it needs to know each of us. Is this part of the foretelling you mentioned yesterday?' Raphael was finishing his second café con leche now and his sentences were growing longer.

'I wish you had been as inquisitive when I was

trying to teach you,' Ava teased. 'I have already made peace with my ancestors,' Ava exaggerated. She had not; she still harbored a complaint about their lack of accuracy. 'I am quickly learning that the foretelling, the stories we have carried through the generations, they only contained clues, nothing more. The foretelling only told of the flower, and the elixir. But you two, and now the dream, I did not expect.'

Raphael gave her an accusing look.

'Yes, I know, I had expectations,' Ava said, reading his mind. 'Do not remind me.' And then, turning to Miri, she added, 'In the dream this morning, Miri...' Ava's voiced became urgent. 'Did you feel a force or a presence that should not have been there?'

'Raphael was there.' Miri tried to lessen Ava's obvious concern. She was particularly pleased with her morning tease. Raphael was not. Nor was Ava. Ava glared at Miri's angel.

'No. Nothing like you describe,' Miri said, recoiling and shook her head. 'The dreams are always full of surprise. Each night there are similar elements and new and different ones. Last night, Raphael and I were walking in a forest surrounded by butterflies. I remember now, you only arrived at the end of my dream, Ava. Just before I woke, I knew you were troubled and I sensed you awaken.'

Ava looked at Raphael.

'I do not remember the dreams, Grandma, none of them,' he confirmed. 'We were in a forest surrounded by butterflies?!' Raphael repeated. 'Together?' He was impressed and decided to enjoy both the idea and his third café con leche in silence.

'I heard your music in the dream, Miri,' Ava said, softening. 'Now I know why you dance.'

'I sense your concern, Ava. What happened in the dream? What did you see?'

'There was a visitor,' Ava began. 'Someone, an *espira*, like a spy, is watching you.' Ava waited for a reaction.

Miri could not offer one.

'Whatever I felt, it was not the flower. Whatever it is, it did not belong in the dream, does not belong in our world. But it was searching and it was looking at you, Miri. Only you.

'I tried to stay and watch. I tried to follow. The energy was strong, powerful. It was always looking at you Miri, and yet it did not find what it was looking for. And then I felt its intention and I had to wake and wake you too.' Ava paused; she did not hide her distress. 'You see the future, Miri. So you may already know what I will say. Something that wishes you harm is close, and yet it is not near. The presence has been following you for a long time. Whatever it is seeking, it believes you possess it.'

'The flower?' offered Raphael; he was alert now. 'That is the only treasure we have been carrying. What did you see, Grandma? What would it want with the flower?'

'When I entered the kitchen, I thought the same, Raphael. And then I breathed the scent. The scent is the same as the dream. The flower was the dream. We were invited into the dream, by the flower, that is the only reason we were there.

'But this force had the power to enter the dream, uninvited. And, therefore, could also have taken the dream. It could have taken the essence of the flower while it was in the dream. No, it was not even aware of the flower. Only Miri. I am not even sure it sensed me or you, Raphael. It was only following Miri, and followed Miri into her dream, not ours. It is not searching for the flower.'

Ava was troubled and tried to calm with a second café con leche.

'There is nothing in the history of this moment, in anything that has been passed down to me, that mentions a spirit or a monster. The force I felt was not clean, Miri. It meant you harm and means you harm. But I cannot tell you any more. I only know of flowers, not monsters and spirits. But now, since it has entered the dream, the flower also carries the memory, or touch of this force, this monster. Beware a creature with four horns, Miri.' Ava finished and asked Raphael to brew a fresh pot of coffee.

Miri did not need to ask how Ava knew. Miri was learning to see with her own angels. Ava was blind, and yet Ava could see. Miri wanted to see.

When Raphael returned to the table with fresh pots

of coffee and hot milk, 'Let's not speak any more of monsters, Grandma.' Raphael tried to make light of the threat. 'Otherwise, Miri will never walk the Camino again.'

'You are wise, sometimes,' Ava conceded. 'Now pack your mochila and leave if you do not like my hospitality or my conversation, Raphi; do your friends still call you Riff Raff?'

Watching Raphael's scorned face, Miri joined Ava's laughter.

'So you are Riff Raff?' Miri piped. 'I heard some gossip on the Camino of someone called Riff Raff who joined the communal dinner in a *donativo* albergue without his shirt. Topless.'

Ava encouraged Miri. 'Topless? Who goes to a communal dinner in an albergue topless?'

Miri continued laughing. 'The young women had a lot to say about his body!'

'Have you no shame, young man?' Ava was enjoying the moment.

Raphael was not used to women pouring embarrassment upon him and could not find the drain.

'I was washing my clothes! I had nothing to wear!' He protested, hiding his face behind his fresh café con leche.

'I completed the book last night, Ava. I leave the flower and the book with you. Will you make the elixir today?'

Ava looked at Miri curiously. 'I have not read a

book in a long time. Is it about love? What happens at the end of the story?'

'At the end there is a fire, a death, the pain of love, the grief that follows the loss of love, and a new life.'

'The flower you bring also has five senses. The flower contains the energy of the fire, the fire I feel every day, the fire of the sun, and the energy of the moon and the stars which I have felt but never seen. Since the moment you picked the flower, the flower has been trapped inside a memory of the moment of its death. I have sensed much death and yet I have never seen it. From the scent and the sense that I feel, I can tell that the flower is the colour of life, the sunrise and sunset, but I have never seen those either.

'By inviting you into its dreams, the flower has felt your love and it has absorbed all the hidden love inside you, the love offered to you, including that denied or rejected by you. Love, my dear, once given can never be ungiven. You may deny it, push it away. You may think your heart was broken. But the love given remains within you. The flower has absorbed all the love you have touched. Including the love you cast out, rejected, chosen not to see or feel.

'The scent of the flower contains life, death, grief, love and a fire. Since you have kept it in a book, the scent and the oil will be in the book, and I must have the book too. You must return and tell me the ending of the next book, the sequel.'

'I do not know if there is a sequel, Ava.' said Miri.

'This story you have told me sounds like it will have a sequel, and will last forever,' said Ava.

'Why is the flower listening, Grandma?' Raphael sensing the flower, looked towards the book.

'Yes. My moment with the flower began when you first opened the gate, yesterday,' Ava confirmed. 'I was not only talking to you yesterday, Miri, I was introducing myself to the flower.'

Raphael raised his eyebrows.

'I am old; I have very little time. You arrived on the night of the alignment of the five beings in the sky. And somewhere else in the world, the moon has crossed paths with the sun leaving behind a ring of fire. An announcement, to those who wish to see, that the flower of the silent heart has arrived.'

'Your bedtime stories were not stories at all, were they?' Raphael recalled, a little perplexed. 'What else can you tell us about the flower, Grandma?'

27

The Flower

'The flower is called the "The Silent Heart".

'The story begins when an angel died. Angels cannot die. And yet this angel, who was sent to teach the first kings, the first humans, about law, justice, creating a good community on Earth, died. The people who knew the angel, and came to love the angel, grieved and buried the body. That is another story for another time. A flower, the first of its kind, with a colour and shape of a human heart, grew upon the grave of the angel. And only upon the grave. The flower became known as The Silent Heart.

'With time and over a thousand generations, the knowledge of the flower became a tale, passing into children's legends and myths told by storytellers. While some tales spoke of a power inside a mysterious flower, the true memory of the flower was secretly collected, treasured and protected by a community that came to be known as the flower collectors. But time also has a way of breaking the very memories it creates. One by one, as flower collectors passed, and then lines of flower collectors took their knowledge of the flower with them, many pieces of the memory of the flower of the silent heart was erased in their passing. The remaining pieces of memory have been passed down to me, through my family, the last of an ancient line of flower collectors.

'According to those who came before me, the potion we will prepare is called the Elixir of The Silent Heart. The only knowledge of the elixir passed to me, as well as the making of the elixir, is that the potion will wake a silent heart.

'The meaning of the words, waking a silent heart, has been lost. So I cannot tell you the purpose of the elixir, I can only repeat the words given to me. I cannot tell you who the elixir is for, who will benefit, when, or how. I cannot even tell you how the elixir will reach the one for whom it will be made. If the answer was known by my predecessors, it is not part of my knowledge.

'If I am honest, what will happen after I have made the elixir, and the thought of who the elixir will benefit, has not preoccupied me till now. If there is a clue in the knowledge passed to me, I seek it tonight.

'But I do know that the making of the elixir is the last piece of knowledge I have left in my body and my mind, and it will be my last offering to this world. Now that you have brought the flower, Miri and Raphael, we will complete the fulfilment of a knowledge carried by generations of flower collectors in my family.'

'Is it not strange, Grandma, to make an elixir and not know what it will do?' Raphael knew that every one of Ava's elixirs had a purpose.

'I have no idea how, or even if, the elixir will

change the course of one life, or more. Maybe no one will be touched by the elixir that I will make. I have no idea what the magic will do. I would like to believe that the waiting has had a purpose, and that the elixir will touch the whole world, maybe, if I am truthful, I would like it to touch all the worlds, the living, the spirits, the angels, the entire universe of beings. I will never know. But I did know that the flower from the ancient stories would arrive at my door.'

'How?' Raphael had to interrupt.

'I knew the day my mother died, Raphael. There was a scent in the forest where she died. More than a scent, more than an energy you might feel when you walk into a home, or a forest. When she fell I sensed a mystery, a force. It was beyond all the flowers I had studied with my mother. So I prepared. I prepared by remembering the detail of every story, every piece of knowledge passed to me. Now that we are here, I must admit, all the stories have not been as useful as I might have expected,' Ava giggled. 'Wait till I tell my ancestors.

'I listened to the bird song, the words that came in the winds, my mother's last words. When I understood that the flower was arriving, I also knew I would need every memory of my life to pass on to the flower, to prepare the flower. I did not expect the dream. I did not know that the flower would be inviting you, us, and discovering our lives through its dreams. But in that collection that the flower is now carrying, the collection of our experiences of life, lies the secret to unlocking and releasing the magic contained inside the flower.'

'Wow,' Ava was pleased to hear Raphael exclaim.

Miri wondered why Ava had not yet taken the flower from inside the book. Before she could ask, Raphael continued.

'Not life.'

Ava looked at Raphael's angel. She breathed the scent of the flower again.

'Love,' Raphael said slowly with a knowing smile before Ava could correct herself. 'Not experiences of life. It is listening to our experiences of love.'

28

The First Elixir

'You are constantly surprising me, Raphael. Yes, love. Those who do not understand either, often confuse life and love. And I do not understand either. We will talk of love tonight.

'Today, we will begin with a rehearsal. To make the first elixir, I will need your help, Raphael.'

Raphael looked at his grandma and nodded immediately.

'I could make excuses and tell you that my hands are stiff and weak. That I need your help to measure and mix the ingredients. But now I understand another truth I saw in the dream this morning. And it was not in any foretelling. Miri has carried the flower, but it is you, her companion, who has journeyed the Camino with her, and who has been walking with Miri in the dreams, you are the one who will be the bearer. You will carry the elixir from this house, to the place and time, and maybe even to the one in need. I cannot say how, but you will know, Raphael. In the same way you hear the words of the flower, the elixir, once made, will guide you.'

Raphael nodded. He trusted the moment, and his grandmother. The Camino had already taught him to surrender.

'Today we prepare a special elixir for you. One I have been thinking of preparing for a long time.'

'For me?' Raphael was intrigued and confused.

'With the elixir we make today, you will be able to see your reflection.'

Raphael scoffed as if his grandmother was playing a dark joke.

That is not possible, he wanted to reply. But he did not want Ava to add to his hurt and wounds.

'I can see you are not convinced,' Ava laughed. 'We will practice today by making the elixir for you. But once made, you do not have to use it. Just keep it close, Raphael. One day, you will be ready to see yourself. And when you are ready to look in the mirror, to look inside yourself, you will remember this day, your grandmother, and if you want, you will choose to use the elixir. Raphael, once it is made, use it wisely,' Ava warned.

Raphael looked at Miri.

'You have fallen in love with her,' teased Grandma.

Raphael was not embarrassed within the moment of truth.

'Yes, Grandma, I have.' Raphael continued the elaboration. He felt bold. 'But when the Camino is over, Miri will return to her life and I will not know her any more. She will only be in my memory. And if the elixir can help me see my reflection, then I will know who I am and if I can be loved by someone other than my grandmother.'

Miri should have felt embarrassed, but she was not. She laughed! You are easy to love, she wanted to say. Not in front of Ava, she decided.

'Let's fill our evening tonight with stories of love, great idea, Ava,' Miri agreed, intrigued.

'And in the night, the flower may invite us into one more dream.' Raphael hoped to remember a little more of the dream.

Ava began a list of instructions for Raphael even as they stood. 'Today, you will remember the ingredients again, the tools, the equipment, the measurements and learn to prepare the mixing.'

Miri offered to help but quickly stepped aside to watch the dance. Miri enjoyed the choreography of angels and the dance of love between Raphael and Ava. A choreography that reminded Miri of a rainy morning and the coin collector who had never watched the raindrops dance before.

And when Miri glanced at the book containing the flower, Miri was surprised that the book was engulfed in soft blue, green and yellow flames.

Ava interrupted Miri's gaze. 'Our words are still vibrating in the air, Miri. The flames are absorbing every word of love it can reach. The flower is preparing.'

Miri continued to stare at the flames.

'What do you see?' Ava asked.

'Like angels but different.'

Raphael looked at the book, he only saw the cover. A tree in flames. He shook his head, wondering about the different worlds they shared.

Raphael's elixir was ready by evening.

The kitchen, the equipment, Ava and Raphael filled the house with the satisfaction of a successful rehearsal.

While enjoying the show, Miri prepared a light lunch and a variety of snacks for the evening. Plenty of time for Miri's thoughts to invade her mind. She did not feel special, or important. Ava described her as having some sort of destiny. She understood and accepted Ava's energy. Through Ava, Miri understood angels and their faces and there was no more fear inside her. But she could not accept that the universe, the flower, or Ava had been waiting for her. She was different, Miri knew. Now that Ava had introduced her to her angels, Miri needed to spend time with them. To know them. Everyone is unique and different, she told herself. I am not special, she concluded.

Miri laid her freshly prepared snacks on the table outside. Raphael brought a third chair from the kitchen. The three friends, for they were more than family, sat together on the porch to absorb the last rays of the setting sun surrounded by delicious snacks.

'Miri's Tapas.' Raphael gave the porch a new name.

And even as the sun disappeared leaving the moon in charge of the evening and the night, Raphael described the five heavenly beings lit brightly in the sky.

'Like a little chain of beads coming out of the moon. I have not seen five planets in the sky before,' said Raphael, overwhelmed.

'So there are seven heavenly beings aligned tonight?' Ava counted.

'Yes, of course,' Raphael was grateful for the wisdom. 'The Earth and the moon.'

'Do you think it means anything?' Miri asked.

'When you add the sun, the number is eight.' Ava smiled. 'Seven is creation, eight is completion. Everything has a meaning, a reason. The planets have gathered for the flower. The flower will share our stories of love with the universe tonight. This much, at least, is in the foretelling.'

'What is your story, Grandma?' Raphael could not resist.

29

Ava

'His name was Abrao, your great-uncle. We met in an ashram in Seville, under the shade of an ancient oak tree. A local tradition claims that the tree was planted by a famous philosopher during the time when Emirs and Caliphs ruled what they called Andalusia. According to the story, the philosopher travelled to the holy land where he made a detour to an ancient site called Moreh where it is believed that Abraham built the first altar to his god under an oak tree. The philosopher was so taken by the site that he collected some seeds of the tree and brought them back with him and planted one of them in the garden of what is now an ashram. We would often sit under our tree performing our daily meditations and wondering if the tradition was true. And if we were sitting in the shadow of Abraham.

'One morning, we began the day sitting opposite random partners, looking into each other's eyes, and we would ask the other what they saw inside our hearts.

'I was blind and many people were nervous of sitting opposite me. But he was the only one who saw the light in my eyes; he saw my hearts. I saw his angel.

'He was Italian. From a region called Abruzzo. He arrived in the ashram to make sense of, and make peace with, the violence he had experienced during a foreign posting in the Italian army. We were immediately drawn to one another. We decided to marry even before our time in the ashram had come to an end. But I had no desire to move or to live in a city apartment. When he came to the Meseta, he fell in love with the expanse, the colours, the silence, and I was glad we decided to live in Spain.

'When I was still a child, I did not understand the purpose of my life and what being a flower collector meant. But after the ashram, many people began to approach me with their traumas, and fears and pain. I began mixing the flower elixirs taught to me as a child, with my mother's help, she was still alive, and those who took my potions returned with stories of healing. My new husband accepted my art, my gift, my knowledge of mixing oils and essences. He believed in the healing power of flowers and knew I was healing myself as much as I was healing others. I did not have to explain anything to him.

'But I did not understand love. I still do not. We are always learning to touch that deepest feeling inside us, a sensation that wants to consume us, but we resist. I was scared, maybe we all are scared of love. And yet, love is our purpose. I allowed the fear to decide for me, and that was my mistake in my life and marriage.

'My marriage felt perfect for a long time. But

without my knowing, I lost my husband when I began to think more about my flowers than the love we shared and offered each other. And he lost me when he began working long hours for the money he thought I needed, or wanted, for a larger house with a larger garden with more flowers. Imagine the tragedy.

'I never told him the small house we lived in when we first married was enough. Only when you lose something precious do you realise what you truly crave. Him, his love, was all I truly craved. He died before he could enjoy the money he earned or the freedom of a retirement. We had enough between us to retire early. But we never told each other to pause, or stop, or told ourselves to begin to enjoy our world.

'I feel guilty. But regret and blame does not help or change a truth. We loved, but we could have loved so much more.'

'I do not remember him,' Raphael admitted. 'I was too small.'

Ava's eyes were damp with memories.

'Tears of joy?' Miri already knew.

Ava laughed. 'Crazy, passionate love, actually,' she confirmed.

Raphael cast his eyes to the floor.

'Why does love embarrass you, young man?' Ava admonished.

Raphael looked at Miri.

'I think you have woken his heart, my dear Miri,' Ava teased. 'But there is no one to wake yours.'

If it was Miri's turn to be embarrassed, she did not rise to the invitation.

'I remember the first time he held my hand. Hands that I had wanted to hold me. And every time he touched me, held me, there was nothing, no energy or force to compare. His touch held a powerful force of love that came from deep inside him. His love was sincere, innocent, unpolluted. He quoted some terrible Italian romantic poetry. *"Tu sei bella ragazza come un sole de la matina,"* pardon my Italian.

'He made me laugh. His Italian flirting was exaggerated and yet consuming. He would correct my attempts at Spanish Italian.'

'Sei bella come il sole della mattina...' Raphael tried to play the part of grandfather. He had never heard the story before.

Ava approved.

'We went to Madrid to listen to Helen Shapiro. It was 1967, if I remember, because we married the year after. The Beatles played first; they were the backing band. We kissed the first time in Madrid, after the Beatles played their last song.

'When we first married, every morning when we woke, he would place his hand upon my heart, and I would put my hand over his and close my eyes.'

'So romantic,' said Miri, thinking of her past love. He never did anything like that with her. His touch was nothing special. She missed him less. It was good he was no longer in her life. She still had a lot to learn about love, she decided.

Ava let the silence carry the moment.

'Tell the flower about your love, or loves, Miri. The flower is waiting.'

'I will make some Cola Cao for us.' Raphael's voice confessed to a slight embarrassment. He was never comfortable around the word love.

30

Miri

'Today, sitting with the two of you, sipping this Cola Cao, thanks Raphael, my story feels different to when I began the Camino. Like I am acting in a theatre.

'If everything you say, Ava, is true, I had to live and feel a drama in order to create a reason to walk the Camino, to find Raphael, to find the flower and journey here, to you.

'It was San Lorenzo, I was on campus in Madrid. The night with the highest concentration of falling stars. My astronomy club had gathered on the college plaza to look at the heavens, and as I looked at the star, I began to express my desires and waited for their replies.'

'What did the stars tell you?' Ava asked.

'That love is complicated. Love is not easy.' Miri laughed. 'He was one of the group. I liked him. He spread a blanket on the grass and we lay down together. Later that night when he held me in his arms, I felt his heart, I knew.

'Days became weeks and weeks became months. I discovered that I had already begun to love him with my soul, my body, my mind, my being.

'He would describe how beautiful I was to him. I

kept forgetting to tell him how beautiful he was to me,' Miri laughed. 'We were still young in our increasingly busy and complicated studies and then later with our careers, jobs. For him, maybe it was just an experience, but for me love was a drug. I unleashed every little bit of love inside me and showered him with it. I did not know how to make the right decisions at the right time.

'With him, I felt safe, feeling love was easy, so we decided to live together. I had loved before but this was deeper, different, special, for me at least. And so we talked about marriage. We talked about children.

'And then two words.

'It was not a face that spoke the two words. Two words on Facebook: "Its over."

'Even the grammar was not right.' Miri paused trying not to get angry.

'Two devastating words.

'At the time, it felt as if the sum total of the love I have given him, that we had shared, and he had taken from me, was worth only two words. And two words on Facebook.

'I grieved the love I had lived and given to him in exchange for those two words.

'I grieved for the love given with my heart, and which he had discarded with those two words.

'I had boyfriends before but it was the first time I experienced a broken heart.

'And then, on the Camino, I grieved again when I saw Raphael's angel in Puente la Reina. A memory of a grief for another loss, a forgotten loss. I was petrified at seeing the angel and the memories they ignited.

'But when I met you the second time, Raphael, on that dark morning by the Roman bridge, I understood that your angel was pointing to love. Not just to the love of the past, but the love that was to come.

'I know how it feels to love and be loved. The Camino has helped me understand that the love that I gave and received, all of that love, is inside me and will always remain inside me. That love has become part of my soul. Something beautiful I will always carry. But my heart still hurts.'

'The Camino has taught you much,' Ava said comfortingly.

'Meeting you, Ava, I do not understand. I was not looking for you and yet here I am. I was not looking for the flower, and yet here we are. Seeing you, I realise that when I gave up the world of angels, I gave up myself. My last relationship led me here, it was never meant to last, because I was not myself. He did not know me, the real me. And that is why he had to let me go.

'Because of you, Raphael, I see angels again. Because of you, Ava, I see my angels. I did not even know I had angels. You have both returned me to my life. The life I am supposed to be living. And because of this Camino, I have learnt to see love.'

Gentle tears were falling.

'Tears of regret?' It was Ava's turn.

'Relief!' Miri countered, laughing.

'You are not yet finished with love. And love is not yet finished with you, Miri.' Ava comforted her.

Raphael smiled too. He loved his grandma. She always knew what to say.

'The scent of the flower has changed,' exclaimed Ava, trying to read the air. She realised Raphael had already heard the flower.

'The flower is ready,' Raphael announced, with both surprise and relief. He would not have to share his tragic disasters of love. 'The flower was waiting for your stories!'

31

Hari

Consciousness.

Hari felt a new awareness of his existence and the space around him.

Hari had always been at one with the universe. But now he was separate. He was alone.

Hari had never felt separate before.

Detached.

Hari looked into the new void around him and wondered what this new moment was. This new feeling of being entirely unconnected, alone. Having never felt alone before, he wondered about the new emptiness that surrounded him.

Hari felt lost.

And the universe is vast to be lost in.

32

Kiss

'The flower is ready. Thank you, Miri and Raphael.' Ava stopped suddenly. She began to look around, unable to hide the commotion inside her.

'What's wrong, Grandma?' Raphael understood she felt unsettled.

'Worry not, I have to retire now.' Ava stood. 'Kiss me good night, both of you.'

Ava's embrace with Miri lingered longer that Raphael's.

'Visit me tonight, Miri,' Ava invited. 'I want to teach you how to see the world through your angels.'

Miri and Raphael remained in the night, staring at the sky. Raphael tried very hard to hide his intense desire to kiss Miri.

Miri already knew about the kiss.

Maybe Miri made it easy for him. But they found themselves stepping into a lingering kiss that grasps hold of a heartbeat as it merges with the flowing soul. Miri felt Raphael's arms around her. At the end of the sensation, when Miri opened her eyes and saw Raphael's angel, she knew his words before they came,

'I have never felt a kiss like that before.'

Miri's body consumed the touch, the way Raphael wrapped his arms around her, his lips and fingertips on her skin, the way he caressed her back. His embrace completed her. As if her body had been waiting for him, waiting for his touch. The feeling and sensations were new, unexpected.

Your words are filling my heart, Miri wanted to say. Instead, she replied, 'I do not know of elixirs and remedies, Raphael. Your elixir. Ava said that you will see your reflection, see yourself, that you will know who you are. But one thing I have already seen, you are already loved. You love, and your grandmother consumes your love.'

'I do not understand everything Grandmother says,' Raphael admitted. 'Her senses are stronger than mine. She, and you, see a world that I cannot. My grandmother and the flower were waiting for you. I do not understand the story we are recreating here. I do not know my purpose or what I will do with the elixir she has made today. But she has made it for me, so I will keep it. She has never made an elixir for me before.' Raphael chuckled. 'It will be a memory, like a talisman. A small amount of liquid filled with every memory I have of her. Maybe I will use it one day. Maybe not.'

Raphael wanted to feel the "Oh my God" moment again. So he gently caressed and kissed her again.

The kiss.

'Grandma is convinced that I will know where to take the elixir. Really, Miri, I do not know of elixirs.

This world you two share, is not mine. To me, the flowers have been nothing more than Grandma's hobby. If I cannot even see myself, how will I know where and when another is in need of the elixir?'

'Ava told me that she was abandoned by the village because of her lack of sight and her belief in flowers,' Miri replied, trying to put Raphael at ease. 'People called her a magician, some called her witch. She told me that one of your ancestors was burned in Logroño.

'Have faith in your grandma, in the flower. The flower has brought us together and brought us here. I did not know the flower was destined for Ava. I just carried it. It brought me here. Trust the universe. When you carry the elixir, it will bring you where you need to be. You can hear the flower, Raphael. Listen for the voices. The elixir will guide you.'

'These are words about destiny. I do not know anything about my destiny,' Raphael replied. 'But the Camino has taught me to trust the way and to accept.'

Miri had to agree with Raphael. She was not sure that she had any destiny, but she did believe in the Camino.

Later that night, while lying in bed, Raphael lived, slept and dreamt the infinite kiss. A kiss that took him to a place he decided to call heaven.

After her visit to Ava, Miri too remained awake. But it was not her angel that kept her awake, she too felt the kiss on her lips.

The kiss was more beautiful, more powerful than

any other kiss from any other lover. But the kiss also served to wake an unintended memory. She could not bear the responsibility for another heartache.

Miri could not sleep. She could only think of a small black stone with a thin white stripe across the middle. A stone collected from a dry river bed while on a trekking weekend in Aragon with her parents. Hidden in her mochila, the stone felt important. She intended to leave the stone on the Mountain of Burdens. What burdens would she leave behind? Burdens from a past love, of course. So why would she wish to collect new weights, new burdens?

The kiss with Raphael weighed heavily on her.

She was just beginning to learn about her angels. She needed to spend time with her angels.

She did not want to lead Raphael with a kiss and trap him in a cycle of heartbreak and pain. Love seemed to be attached to pain. She did not want his pain to come stumbling upon her, to bury her.

She should not have kissed him. She should not have let him kiss her.

But she also needed to feel the kiss. She needed to know the kiss. That she was desired, could be loved. She needed to be kissed.

She needed. His hands; his touch felt different. Felt perfect.

The next morning, Miri woke one minute before her five a.m. alarm. And Miri packed her mochila. Before securing the top, Miri reached deep inside the mochila and recovered the small black stone with a thin white stripe across the middle. She remembered the valley, her parents, and the moment when she collected the stone. She remembered the love that surrounded her in that moment. The stone was still important. But the reasons with which she had burdened the stone were no longer important.

33

Mistake

Miri's fingers instantly drowned and numbed as they entered the nighttime teardrops resting on the dawn-cold metal gate.

The gate creaked the alarm, reluctant to let Miri leave.

Closing the gate, Miri lifted her dew-kissed fingertips to her lips and her apprehension of leaving quickly transformed into a wicked blush as she thought of Raphael.

Feeling her own angel's presence, Miri looked towards her Camino and into the starlit sky through her angels for the first time in her life. And then she sought Ava's angel.

For the second morning in a row, Ava woke with a start and immediately sensed Miri's egress. Angels do not leave without a farewell.

Ava allowed her angel to follow Miri for as long as Ava's soul would allow, and long enough for their angels to say goodbye. And in that short moment when the angels embraced, Ava sensed the life-giving essence of Raphael's kiss with Miri.

Still half asleep, Ava lost herself in the memories

of her youth, her loves, her kisses, and Ava wondered why she had never walked the Camino. And in that same moment, as Miri's presence dissolved away into a vacant mist, Ava sensed something more in the angel embrace. Ava caught a glimpse which led her to touch the presence of the powerful force that she now understood came from Miri. She allowed herself to feel the force and began to unravel what the monster was seeking.

The sensation carried Ava from the kiss to another place, another life, another memory, another world. Ava was suddenly in the moment of her coming of age. Being welcomed into adulthood.

Ava's mother was telling her a story, her story. They were in a forest. A special time in her life when, for a whole lunar month, Ava spent every day and some nights in the forests around their home and in northern Spain with her mother. Some days were silent; other days were filled with stories, and every day her mother introduced her to new flowers. Under the sun-spotted cool of the leaves, she learnt about the line of flower collectors from the time of the expulsion from Spain, the same year as the discovery of the new land in the West.

Through every story and every flower, she learnt the secrets of the forests and the magic hidden inside the flowers. Amongst the stories was the ancestor who was burned as a witch and the mystery of the flower of the silent heart, the flower all her ancestors had waited all their lives for. She also learnt about the elixir that would be made from the flower, and she learnt about angels.

It was during one early morning sojourn in a forest near Roncesvalles, she accepted her lack of sight. Until then she had fought her eyes. She had battled with other people's sight, wanting to see the same as them. But in the forest, she found she could smell the trees, the flowers, and the memory of her senses was no different to the memory of seeing. She found flowers from their scent before her mother did; she found her way out of the dark forest from the smell of a leaf or a tree, and that was when she began to see different kinds of light, another sense she had not allowed herself to see before. She met her angels for the first time in the forest and her angels taught her to see the flowers, the trees, the grass, and even the sky and the stars with their eyes.

And when Ava saw light for the first time in her life, she already knew it was not a light anyone else around her could sense or see.

The light was not the light from the sun, but from an experience of life. The light of all love in the world.

Ava called it the time of her awakening.

Every year, on the day before the last full moon of the lunar cycle, Ava and her mother visited the forest. Her last visit was almost twenty years ago. The day her mother died. Ava remembered being in the forest and suddenly being surrounded by little lights she thought were stars. She asked her mother to describe them, through her eyes.

'Cabbage white butterflies,' her mother said. And

Ava danced with the butterflies. And it was during the dance that Ava felt a new presence.

The awareness of the new force that lasted less than a heartbeat, but it almost took her breath away. She always remembered the sensation in her body of that presence, the force, for it was during the dance that her mother fell, and never stood again.

When the vision ended, Ava opened her eyes to the comfort of her pillow but to a new and unexpected alarm. Ava calmed herself to be sure of her realisation before lifting her frail body with her frail arms and sat at the edge of her bed.

The same presence she felt in Miri had been in the forest when her mother died.

She was sure.

And so she realised her error.

When her feet touched the floor she sensed the absence.

At first, Ava thought that Miri had taken the book and the flower. That she was sensing the loss of the flower. But the scent of the flower reassured her it still lay in the kitchen, still in between the pages of the book.

The vacancy in the house was not the leaving of Miri, it was the memory of the missing force, the light that Miri had been carrying and which Ava had failed to recognise.

Miri had been in the forest the day Ava's mother had died.

'Wake up,' Ava cried from her bedroom, tears for

her mother still drying in her eyes.

She rushed to Raphael's bedroom door and tapped loudly with her walking stick.

'I have made an error, Raphael. Forgive me. We have all made a mistake.' She knocked again more desperately. 'We must prepare the elixir now. Adesso.'

Raphael opened the bedroom door sleepily, 'What is wrong, Grandma?' assuming another one of his grandma's dramas until he saw her wet face. 'What's wrong?'

'It was never the flower, Raphael, dear.'

Raphael was confused but always knew that his grandmother's words would eventually make sense.

'Miri is in danger. She is being followed.'

Raphael was still waking but the word "danger" apprehended him.

'Yes, the monster, you told us yesterday.'

'Raphael, listen. It was never just the flower,' Ava tried, but Raphael was still not fully awake. 'Wash; I will make coffee, then come to the kitchen quickly. I will explain.'

Fresh café con leche. Raphael felt the comfort but the comfort did not last long.

'Where is Miri?' Raphael expected the commotion to have woken her.

'She left, Raphael. Before the sun.'

Ava sensed his urgency and disappointment.

Raphael glanced out of the window. The sun had already risen and was over the trees. He had a fleeting impulse to run after Miri but he already knew she was too far away.

Ava paused, waiting for the question that did not come.

'She left because of the kiss, Raphael.' Ava was impatient.

The words hurt. He never ceased to wonder how his grandmother read his thoughts, knew his secrets, and was the reason he felt relief when he eventually left the house to begin his university course in Milano.

'Let her walk. You have touched her soul. She is already confused. Give her time.'

The advice did not stop Raphael wanting to be with Miri.

'That is the problem, Raphael. You want. Stop wanting. Start accepting.'

He was still confused. But Raphael knew not to fight his grandma's words. She was right, of course. Miri had to find her own Camino.

'I need you to wake and concentrate. To listen to my words. Your elixir is ready. It is in the phial on the table.'

Raphael tried to calm himself with another sip of the soothing café con leche. In the middle of the table sat a small cylindrical clear glass phial. The silver lid was attached to a black thread, long enough to fit around his neck. It looked like a talisman. He stared at the liquid as he finished his coffee and then lifted it to inspect the phial more closely.

'I did not expect the elixir to be yellow. It was without colour last night.'

Inspecting the magical serum, his attention was caught by the two wings that spanned out of the lid. The lid was the shape of an angel. He loved the bottle as much as the love in the elixir.

'The liquid is the colour of the sun?' Ava raised her eyebrows. 'When I poured and held the elixir, it felt like the sun's warm rays on a cloudless summer day.' Ava smiled. 'The elixir takes the colour of the moment, Raphael.'

'I will be able to see my reflection with this potion? I will see myself?' Raphael thought out loud, not entirely convinced.

'Only if you believe, and only if you are ready will you see your soul, Raphael,' Ava explained.

'You said Miri is in danger?' Raphael asked, more alert now but more calmly.

Ava had been waiting.

'It is far more complicated than I believed, Raphael. Imagine, I have been waiting for this moment all my life and we did not even know what we were waiting for. I am still trying to understand. Forgive me if I do not make sense. My thoughts are moving fast.

'Miri's life is in danger.' Ava spoke slowly, as if reading a page already written in her mind. 'And now, I understand why. You and I will make the elixir of the silent heart, that is my purpose. When the elixir is ready, you will carry the elixir with you and return to the

Camino. Miri will be some days ahead of you. If you walk fast, and I know you will, you will catch up with her. By then, Miri will know what the kiss meant to her.'

'Tell me about the danger, Grandma?' It was Raphael's turn to be impatient. He poured more coffee and hot milk for the two of them.

'My entire life, my mother, grandmother, her mother and all the flower collectors that have passed before, have waited for the secret flower of the silent heart. We waited for the flower to arrive so we could make the elixir. But somewhere along the line, the piece of knowledge relating to the bearer of the secret flower has been erased, forgotten. Today, I am seeing the flower bearer for the first time and am realising the mistake of my forbears. A mistake I must put right. I *must* put that right.'

Ava paused to calm down. She sipped her coffee.

Raphael waited.

'Miri carries something special, Raphael. Something not of this world. A very powerful force that does not belong here, but another realm. Having met Miri, and her angel, I can tell you that she is not aware of the presence of the force or the power she possesses.'

'This force, Grandma. I did not see or sense anything. Why is it important?'

'I did not recognise the force till this morning. The force comes from another world, a place of creation. It may even be the essence of creation itself, from a place where souls know each other. A force of goodness.

Imagine, a force that creates life. So powerful, that in the wrong hands, the force has the capacity to destroy life, all life.'

Raphael found it difficult to comprehend such a force. He listened more intently. He had not sensed anything unusual in Miri. How was Miri's life in danger? What did he have to do?

'Everything I was taught — we flower collectors were taught, about the flower of the silent heart, was one part of the story. The flower was easier to remember, I suppose,' Ava laughed.

Raphael smiled too. Ava's humour. 'The flower bearer?' Raphael repeated Ava's earlier words and his eyes widened as he began to understand. He sat up, stared at his grandma's face, lit by the low morning sun.

'We always believed we were waiting for the flower, the secret flower, a flower that would only be seen by one who has seen an angel. But the flower too was waiting. That the flower found Miri is no accident. That you were with Miri is no accident. It was never the flower. Do you understand? The flower was waiting for Miri. Miri is the secret of the flower. Miri *is* the story.'

Raphael was having trouble processing the words. Too much information before completing his second café con leche.

'She is the special one you have been waiting for! All these years!'

He began to understand.

'The danger, Grandma. Tell me about the danger. I

have to warn Miri. I can text her. I can ask her to return.'

'There is a being that follows Miri. The being is not from this world, Raphael, and intends to take the force she carries. During the taking, Miri will be harmed. I sense the danger. The flower, the Camino, your bringing her here with the flower, it all makes sense now. *You* collected Miri. You are the Flower Collector, not me.'

Raphael did not hear, or chose not to understand, the last part. All he wanted to do was run after Miri and bring her back.

'No, Raphael. While she is on the Camino she is safe. She heard my words. She carries my warning. And when she faces the monster, only one thing will save her.'

'The elixir?' Raphael finally put the pieces together, his eyes wide. 'That is why she came here. So you can know her and make the elixir that will keep her safe.'

'Not just safe. Miri's life depends on the elixir, and on you reaching her before the monster, whatever this monster is. You must be with her when she faces the monster. When the moment arrives, only the elixir will save her.'

'Tell me more about this force she carries, Grandma. I could not feel anything when I was close to her.'

'It is a power not of this world, Raphael. That is why you cannot sense it. The one who possesses the force will decide the future of all human kind. It is a power that creates love, life. But the same power can destroy all love. The power to destroy life, to change our world, Raphael.'

'You are scaring me, Grandma. You are describing something terrible. You are describing an end to the world, an Armageddon I once read of in the holy books. You know I grew up ignoring your visions because I never understood them. But I have always known that everything you say is true. And now, because I hear the flower, I also feel the meaning of the words you describe.'

Ava paused, allowing the consequences of what they were about to do to sink into Raphael's soul. He had to understand, and believe.

'Today, the visions are clear, Raphael. Let the magic of the Camino embrace her and keep her safe. If you run to her now, Raphael, without the elixir, you will be of no help to her.'

Raphael nodded; he was listening to the flower. 'The flower had to be carried by Miri, had to absorb Miri's heart, her feelings, her experience, her love; the moment of her birth, the deep love of her childhood; her life. Now the flower is ready. So that when the elixir is made, the elixir would read her hearts, enter her hearts, join with her, become part of her life force, and protect Miri.'

Ava could not have said it more clearly. She allowed Raphael the silence so he could listen to his voice, to the flower.

When Raphael nodded again, Ava replied, 'I had no idea, until now, what it means that you are the bearer, Raphael. You speak to the flower. When you carry it, the elixir will absorb your experiences, your life and your love, especially the love you feel for Miri, Raphael. I had no idea that you would be the last ingredient!'

Raphael did not like the idea of being an ingredient, but his grandmother's words, like a puzzle, fitted together, made sense.

'Let's begin, Raphael. You will carry the elixir to her. You cannot tell her what I have told you. Do not scare her when you see her again. Miri does not know the power she carries. That is the only explanation for her presence here and for this story we are living. If she knows, the knowledge may harm her. Those who mean her harm may reach her sooner.'

'You are inviting me into a world I do not see or understand, Grandma.'

'I do not know what you will find when you reach Miri. I do not know whether your love for Miri will last, or whether it will be a small moment of love in your life, and if you will grieve when it is lost. But when you are with Miri again, allow the elixir to feel the weight, the kiss and the sensation it brings to your body; listen to your body, listen to your heart, listen to the moment around you. This is important. Listen. For when the moment arrives, you will know what to do with the elixir.'

'You describe a world where a spirit means to

possess a force Miri carries, and intends to harm her, and will not stop until the force is possessed. The elixir we make today from this one unique flower is the key to keeping Miri alive.' Raphael had to check his thoughts and emotions. He also had to abandon them. 'I am ready, Grandma. Let's make the elixir. And I am scared. What if...' Raphael trembled. '... I make a mistake? There is only one flower.'

'Why do you worry? We rehearsed yesterday. Our family have been practising for five hundred years.' Ava chuckled as they stood there. 'Now describe the feelings you have for Miri,' Ava asked, reaching for the book and the flower.

'Like I have to be next to her. I just want to be close to her. As if she is the only person in the entire world.'

'And the weight, do you feel the heaviness of that feeling?' Ava held the book to her chest and breathed in the air around her.

'I carry no mochila and yet, you are right, a heavy weight is deep inside me.' Raphael began clearing the breakfast pots and readying the worktops and the table for the preparation, almost as if he wanted the distraction.

'Love is heavy. Love is the mystery that connects the life force of your soul with the divine energy in the universe. It is the divine energy that has guided you and brought us together. Feel this new weight of your soul. It is a soul discovering and packing itself with love. You are young, Raphael, and love is waking inside you. Love is what you were born for. Embrace everything you feel when you think of Miri, Raphael.

'The journey of love is greater and much more powerful than the journey of the Camino. But I have not walked the Camino. And you were not ready till now to embrace love.'

'I kissed her, Grandma. And it was like nothing else in the world.' Raphael finished, surprised and a little embarrassed at the confession.

Ava was still holding the book to her chest.

'You say you do not understand my world,' Ava teased. 'But you entered the world of love easily enough!' Ava smiled as she stood.

Raphael watched Ava return the unopened book to the kitchen table, step to the flower cupboard and, with perfect precision, began collecting the bottled ingredients needed for the elixir. Raphael leapt up, dashed to his bedroom and returned with his phone to find a line of bottles next to the book. 'I am going to write the instructions, Grandma.'

'Bring the flower,' Ava began.

'No. You should be the first to touch the flower after Miri, Grandma. Not me.'

'Listen to the flower and listen to the truth of the moment, Raphael. Your part in this story is not an accident. You will be the one to make this elixir, Raphael. Today, I am here to show you, teach you. I have been mistaken in so many ways. I thought, having no children of my own, I would be the last. But it seems,

Raphael, my love, *you* will be the flower collector after me.'

'Nothing makes sense, Grandma. But can you smell the flower? I hear the words of permission. The flower wishes to be set free from its burden.'

'I do not remember a male flower collector in the family. Wait till I meet our ancestors.'

'Was there a dream last night; I do not remember?' Raphael wondered.

'No,' Ava replied, remembering. 'There was no dream last night. I only sensed the monster, Raphael.'

34

The Creature

Hari sensed a new moment. He sensed time, he sensed a "before".

And in this new moment, in his new present, he heard something beyond the songs of the universe: he heard the sound of the words of the Camino.

Now he knew why the Camino was stronger than himself, beyond him; the Camino was a powerful language. A language he did not understand, he could not understand. A language beyond his being. A language of love only experienced through life. Spirits cannot understand love, or life.

And so the Collector of Burdens turned to his collection of burdens. And when Hari stepped into his before, he found a battlefield of burdens full of suffering and violence, battle and war.

Even if Hari did not know suffering, or violence or war, Hari was a spirit, not a warrior. But Hari knew where to find a warrior.

Hari stepped through the moments of his existence until he came face to face with an ancient creature he had known from his before. A creature, who had once been the greatest and most feared warrior the living world had ever known.

Hari no longer bowed to humans.

Hari no longer bowed to life.

Hari was no longer limited by songs. Hari created his own song. And his song woke and summoned the creature. A creature who had battled many forces since the beginning of spirit kind and the memory of human kind.

Having refused the oath, Hari was no longer chained to serve an existence called life. Hari called upon the creature to battle. To battle with Miri, and to carry her away from the language of the Camino. Far enough away, he told the creature, so that Miri would no longer be inside the protection of the Camino, and there, Hari would approach Miri, collect her burdens and her mystery.

Hari looked towards the force contained in the fist of Miri's left hand. The mystery would be his. And once his, Hari would use it and destroy the purpose of creation, the experience of life, love and time.

The waking creature listened to Hari. A spirit was commanding him. And the creature was pleased to be woken, pleased to fight one more battle.

In the plains of the western regions, the creature had once fought Hercules. And before Hercules, in the forest of Eden, the same creature fought Gilgamesh.

It was not the size of the creature that gave it strength. Strength came from within the being of the creature. The creature was fearless, and that was the seat of its power. And further, in accordance to the myth that the creature stepped into, it was able to appear in any form.

But having only ever lived inside a storm of violence, the creature knew no victory, only battle, and war and death, for there is no victory in battle, or war or death.

Once awoken, and just as Hari had intended, the creature's gaze was drawn, like a firefly's would, towards Miri. The mark of the angels had drawn the creature before, but, for the first time, the creature was taken aback by Miri's power, a weapon he had never seen before.

And it was not the force in Miri's hand the creature saw. It was the four faces of love. Four angel faces. Each face occupied a heart. And she had four hearts. The vision mesmerised the creature. And that Miri was oblivious to the force, the power, the strength she bore, mesmerised the creature even more.

A power unrealized. A power the creature recognised as a weapon beyond any he had faced before. A weapon from another realm, beyond Hercules, beyond Gilgamesh.

To defeat Miri, the creature needed to know the power of the weapon Miri carried. The creature had never seen the realm of love before. And here the creature saw four realms. Four stepping stones to love. And so the creature followed Miri across the Meseta, studied his adversary. The creature learnt her gifts, and sought her weakness.

The creature had seen much evil and it never tired of meeting evil. And the evil continued to shock the creature even though no moment was ever the same. The shock was never the evil itself, but that in every moment, the evil returned and was always the same, always dressed in a new face, a new body, a new armour, with new weapons. Evil that abuses, imprisons, murders and terrorises.

And no matter how much evil he defeated and escorted away from the world, taking it far away, to the seventh firmament, a place so far away from the goodness of life so that the beauty of life would not be tarnished, evil always reappeared in the next moment.

'Will the evil never end? Is evil endless?' the creature had once asked.

But Miri's power was different. Power of goodness and healing and love instead of battle and war and death.

Why had he been chosen to fight such a powerful being?

Miri was not evil, but then nor was Gilgamesh, nor Hercules.

But Miri was more powerful than any previous adversary.

Having been tasked to take Miri away from the Camino, a task the creature had accepted and was now bound to fulfil, the creature knew only one way to defeat his adversary.

To kill.

Being in Spain at the time of the bull runs in Pamplona, the creature would appear to Miri as a bull, a bull with four horns, one to strike each of her hearts. The creature chose his battleground carefully. A dark place. An empty place.

The creature chose a tunnel, under the earth. Where none could come to her defence. From where Miri could not flee.

The creature would wait in the tunnel of Garim.

35

Meseta

The Camino does not wait.

Miri's feet could not wait either. As Miri stepped away, Miri sensed the embrace of the flower collector's angel and she smiled her embarrassment. The short farewell allowed the guilt of her quiet absconding to lessen, but not leave her hearts. She hoped that Ava understood. She hoped that Raphael would too.

She was glad to be walking again. Closing her eyes for a moment she reached into herself and touched the rhythm of her Camino again. She felt the kindling of the sunrise behind her and when she opened her eyes, surprised herself at the depth of the darkness veiling the way ahead. She felt her feet gently caress the cold sleeping earth. She felt the freedom of the Meseta open in front of her. The flashing lights of wind turbines on hills in the far distance to her left and right attempted to measure the expanse around her. Nowhere to hide your story, and she did not want to hide any more.

A familiar sight at a crossroads ahead of her carried Miri to a memory with Raphael. The moonless night had caught a pilgrim at a junction of three road options and Miri watched a torch beam slicing the night, seeking the lost yellow arrow. Reaching the desperate beams, Miri joined the search. Walking ahead a little, Miri spotted a small arrow on a signpost behind an overgrown bush.

'This way,' she called.

'Thanks,' came the voice. 'Keitaro.'

'Miri.'

The dawn on the Meseta is like the waiting for the next kiss; Miri could not help but seek metaphors when the sun finally rose and gently touched awake the cereal fields. She could not help but wonder what it would be like to gently wake next to Raphael. His touch, his kiss, had reached inside her. Why did she not stay?

Soon the dawn sky melted away and the sun lit the colours to reveal the completed painting of the Meseta.

I thought the Meseta was supposed to be barren and bare. Miri marvelled at the colours and the views around her.

'It is not the Meseta that is bare,' Keitaro replied. 'The Meseta lays you bare.'

Keitaro's angel was sharper, brighter than any she had seen before. And when Carmen and Aurora began walking with them, Miri thrilled at all the new pilgrim angel faces, realising that she had stepped into a new Camino. Miri was mesmerised by the spectacular new energy revealing itself around her.

Ava had taught her to see.

The pilgrims' angels were no longer faces.

Miri was witnessing an energy of existence she had never imagined. Is this the energy of life? Miri wondered, every time a new angel face arrived.

Pilgrims do not look behind them. Miri did not look behind her. Had Miri looked, she would have seen another energy.

A bull with four horns.

36

León

Raphael joined the Camino two full days behind Miri. Raphael walked an extra five kilometres, and sometimes more each day to catch up with Miri. But he did not realise he would have to cross the entire Meseta before reaching her. The Meseta made it easy for Raphael to remember his grandmother's instructions. Every time he thought of Miri, he followed his feelings deep inside his body and his mind. He reread his words in the notes app from the night in Cirauqui, and explored the meaning of each word, the feeling of each word. And when the new bottle of elixir around his neck, the elixir of the silent heart, changed colour along the way, he recognised that his heart was opening and he sensed a new gratitude. The elixir was listening. On the Meseta, Raphael learnt to listen to the elixir. And in listening, Raphael felt a freshness inside his mind and realised, for the first time in his life, he had let go of the sadness and anger and pain of his youth. The feelings he had carried all these years, had been left behind. He was listening to his feelings, the now, for the first time. Feelings of love, scared to surface before, were now soaking his skin.

I do not need to see myself any more, he said to

himself.

'Not yet,' said the elixir.

When Miri walked through the wide open gateway into the *Monasterio de las Benedictinas* she was already tired, sweaty and hot. She was also annoyed at the hours of pavement walking into León that had left the soles of her feet aching. But, at the sight of Raphael in the pilgrims' queue, behind the silent family, all her pain and troubles instantly vanished. Miri ran past ten exhausted and patiently waiting pilgrims to reach Raphael.

Elated at the sight of one another, Raphael and Miri attempted a clumsy kiss. It is hard to embrace with a mochila on your back. Raphael, having already dropped his before joining the queue, helped Miri with her mochila and they embraced again, a hot, sweaty and wet embrace. They did not care their joy was shared by their audience, everyone smiled at them.

'The elixir took two days to prepare, not one,' Raphael tried to explain. 'I walked as fast as I could to catch up.'

Miri did not want to talk. Not yet at least. She wanted to feel Raphael's arms around her. Feeling his angel with her new gifts, Miri was feeling her soul.

'Get a room,' came a familiar voice.

'Sara!' Raphael screamed. *After the Meseta, I do not care much for busy shopping streets and cities*, Miri decided.

Raphael and Miri were searching for a place to eat.

'How is Ava?' Ava was always on Miri's mind.

'Why did you leave?' Raphael did not answer.

Miri stopped in the middle of the pedestrian street and they kissed their replies. The joy of holding each other absorbed them.

And when Miri saw the cathedral, she stepped inside into the shower of the summer evening kaleidoscope that streamed through the bouquet of windows. Miri began to dance in the cathedral. When the cathedral security guards ran after her and tried to stop her dancing, she took her dance outside where all of León gathered to dream with her.

'Why do you dance here?' a little Spanish girl asked, mesmerised by Miri's grace.

'The Meseta taught me to dance. And because San Francisco of Assisi came here during his Camino. I dance with his memory.'

The little girl and her mother laughed and both began dancing with Miri. Soon all of León was dancing, except for the cathedral guards.

Miri and Sara found themselves in adjacent beds in a women's only dormitory at the albergue. Two bunks next to each other, like a large double bed. Embarrassing if you do not know your bed partner. Miri had to momentarily open her eyes to remind herself where she was. She was missing the Meseta. But what she saw caused an unsuspecting flood of warm wet tears to erupt out of Miri. The weeping woke Sara.

'All that water I drank today, all two liters,' Miri

whispered, excusing herself. 'It is coming out. It is a tap, it is a tap!' Miri tried to laugh the tears away.

Sara took Miri's hand and comforted her.

Miri could not share the cause of the tears with Sara.

When Miri had opened her eyes, she saw the face of a new angel. An angel she had never seen before. Not an angel that belonged to Sara or any other pilgrim. Miri saw an angel she did not expect to see, let alone recognise.

This was her angel.

The angel Ava had described to her.

Miri saw her angel for the first time. And the tears of joy, inside her, exploded.

37

Raphael

'You did not ask me why I wept last night, Sara. Thank you.' Miri was deeply grateful.

The group had stopped to enjoy the view over an ancient bridge, once the only bridge out of León, just after the Hostal de San Marcos.

Sara did not reply. But she sensed Miri's need for comfort. Sara already understood that she had witnessed a very personal moment. Miri did not need to explain. There is nothing to explain on the Camino.

A pilgrim's comfort.

Sara and Miri stopped that instant, in the middle of the ancient bridge, and hugged. A long hug. A pilgrim's hug.

Carmen and Aurora turned and did not wish to be left out. They joined in. Keitaro and Raphael caught each other's eyes, laughed, and the whole group hugged together. Glad to be together.

Carmen used the moment to sing. Hearing Carmen's voice, Miri and Sara released one another and began a new dance on the bridge. A dance to the joy of Camino friends.

Desayuno was waiting at La Virgen del Camino but

the stretch of hard pavement out of León weighed heavily on the pilgrim feet. A little distance after the café, at an option to step away from the highway and onto a country track towards Villar de Mazarife, the mood and the feet began to calm.

Raphael had been waiting to share his story with Ava.

'The elixir took longer. There was a lot of mixing and a lot of pauses to allow the mixtures to settle. During our pauses, Grandma taught me how to make new healing infusions and special elixirs.' Raphael did not hide his excitement from Miri. 'Pain remedies, in fact remedies for all sorts of ailments, and potions that smell so sweet that Grandma said they would embrace and comfort everyone they touch with just one drop on the back of the hand!'

How do I tell Miri how I feel about her? The weight and words Raphael carried inside his stomach, around his heart, were screaming to escape. *I want to feel my arms around you and don't want to let go,* he kept saying to himself.

If the Meseta had taught him to feel, his mind was quickly learning the language.

Miri saw his angel, saw his words.

The way Miri looked at him, Raphael knew, and felt embarrassed.

'Tell me about your journey,' he said instead.

'Did you see the colours of the Meseta? It took my breath away,' Miri's eyes disappeared into the Meseta.

'The best part of the Camino so far.' She scanned her friends, some ahead, some behind. 'We have laughed and shared crazy truths.'

'I cooked pasta and tuna in an albergue for the group and one day, when he found the ingredients, Keitaro cooked sushi for all of us.' Miri loved his sushi.

Raphael laughed at the impossible thought. Sushi on the Camino? Keitaro was walking next to Raphael, listening. He nodded.

Miri remembered more of her adventures. 'I slept the night under olive trees with two wonderful and beautiful Hungarians. I walked with Giacomo, a counterterrorism officer from Rome. He was in such a rush he only had one sentence for me: "I have to reach Santiago in ten days."'

Keitaro shook his head. 'I remember him. He was planning to walk 45km a day to finish on time.'

'We met Sara from Dublin at a sunset gathering along the Meseta,' Miri continued. 'She remembered walking with you and we have been gossiping about you.'

'Sara is looking for a job and a lover,' Keitaro volunteered.

'Although not in that particular order,' Sara shouted. She was a few steps ahead and her reply drew heaps of laughter.

Raphael was glad to be drawn away from Miri's gossipy comment by Keitaro's intervention and the subsequent laughter.

'I met Carmen and Aurora at the donativo in Mansila de La Mulas. I was struggling with the whole "1 euro for 10 min showers" thing. The coin slot was near the kitchen and the shower was in the dormitory. They helped drop the coin as I entered the shower.' Miri laughed at the crisis. 'We have been walking together, since.

'I practise yoga with Aurora. I love her calm and try to feel her world every time I am with her. And when Alejandro and Felipe began to walk with us, I loved their angels and laughed with the beautiful softness of the love they had to offer.

'I met a pilgrim who had walked the Camino twenty-eight times but he was too much in a rush to talk to anyone. He made me wonder if I will complete the Camino even once!' Miri leaked a slight anxiety. 'But I think I was judging him. Trying to decide if I admired him.'

Keitaro asked Miri to explain.

'When I was little, my mother told me never to tell anyone about the angels that I see. Since I have met all of you I have been sharing my story, describing your angels to you, seeing and sensing your love. There are no witches and no fires here. You accept me, my gift. The first time in my life I am accepted for what I see, what I am.

'I think the Camino teaches us not to judge. Is that possible?'

'The whole world should walk the Camino!'

Raphael had the solution.

Later, when they were walking alone, he told her, 'I walked a little further than usual, each day, to catch up with you.' He described his journey. 'Thanks for the message about the donativo in Mansila de La Mulas. The *voluntario* remembered you and he played the music in the evening just as you described.'

'Did you discover the name of the music?' Miri had left the albergue without asking.

'Butterflies! I will send you the link.' Raphael's hand touched Miri's and he remembered the feeling of the kiss.

'I feel the same, Raphael. Sometimes you do not need to use words. Every touch is a word. The words in your touch, describe mine too. Did Ava tell you about how she sees feelings?' Miri asked, smiling silently at his angel.

Raphael nodded quietly. 'She has been teaching me since I was a child,' Raphael confessed. 'I just never knew. And neither of us realised how much I had absorbed. So when Grandma began to tell me the mysteries, how to measure, sense, feel, mix, know when a potion was ready, how long to wait for each mixture to settle before proceeding, how to touch a flower, how to carry a potion, how to decide the right ingredient, even the stories in my head, everything she tried to teach me as a teenager returned in a moment. Like I already knew!

'While we prepared, Grandma also wanted to know

about the Camino. She asked me to describe my feelings during every moment of every day and every evening and every night.' Raphael saw the intensity in Miri's eyes as he spoke. She was breathing in his every word. Raphael could not remember anyone listening to him, really hearing his voice, before.

'Did you learn the secret of the flower collector?' Miri asked.

'The remedies and the elixir cannot be made without feeling,' Raphael whispered.

Miri smiled. 'You understood. You are closer to her world than you realise, Raphael. You spent a wonderful time with Ava. I am so happy for you.

'So you are the new keeper of her knowledge! She is leaving a very special gift in your care, Raphael.'

'But there is a sadness attached to the gift,' he added, softly. 'She told me that she will not make any more elixirs. She said that she had travelled the Camino through my words and now, with the flower you brought to her, her purpose is complete. I think she was telling me something I did not want to hear. That I may not see her again.'

Miri did not reply.

'The two bottles around your neck?' Miri asked.

'The yellow is for me. I think it looks like the light caramel that they put on the biscuits in Milano.

'The *azzurro*, green and blue, depending on the light and time of day, depending on the stories and feelings I carry to sleep or wake with, is from the flower you collected. The flower of the silent heart. Grandma was surprised with the colour of the elixir. She was not surprised when it began changing colour after I put it round my neck.'

Miri asked Raphael to stop walking for a moment so she could examine the two phials around his neck.

'I am intrigued, Raphael. Now that you have your elixir, the elixir to see yourself, will you take it?'

Raphael looked at Miri but no words arrived. Even if he had wanted to reply, she did not give him the opportunity.

'I have not looked in the mirror since I started the Camino, Raphael. There are no mirrors in the albergues. I do not think any pilgrim can see themselves any more. And yet we see each other. Look at each one of us. I cannot say how I look, but look at them, they look so good, well, healthy, happy, pretty and handsome, smiling. No one is using make up, everyone is waking on bunk beds, sharing toilets and showers. The clothes. We are washing and wearing the same clothes every day. Each morning we dress without mirrors and leave the albergue. What condition we are in and what we look like, it does not matter to us, it does not matter here. Because we accept each other as we are.

'I have spent my whole life looking in mirrors. I know what I look like. I used to worry what I look like. In my other life, I was listening to others tell me what I should look like. Everyone wants to give me their opinions on what I look like or should look like, how I should cut my hair, style my hair.

'If I see my reflection now, I know what will happen. The mirror will show me my life before the Camino, and I do not want to return to that me again. After this Camino, I might remove every mirror in my apartment. I am not sure I want to look at myself again. I have never felt so content about my appearance before. Look at the beautiful people we are surrounded by. Maybe, for the first time in my life I am content, and the truth is, I have not seen myself since St Jean Pied de Port.'

Raphael enjoyed Miri's description. He found it touching and moving. He smiled with his reply.

'I find you very beautiful, Miri. And I am very attracted to you. But you can see yourself in the mirror whenever you choose to. I have never seen my reflection. I want to know what I look like. I want to know what you see when you look at me.'

'And if you are not happy with what you see in the mirror?' Miri persisted.

'Maybe I will look at the mirror once. Once I know what I look like I will carry on being who I am.'

Miri laughed at Raphael's innocent reply.

'You will always be who you are,' Miri struggled to explain. But she also understood that Raphael was on his own Camino of discovery. 'What I am trying to say is, do not be disappointed if the remedy does not work, Raphael.' She tried to prepare him. 'When I am home, I use the mirror every morning. And now, the Camino has made me realise, I have never seen myself, only a face I was trying to hide behind.'

It was Raphael's turn to laugh at Miri's answer. He knew what she meant. 'Maybe I will not take the elixir! I will just keep it around my neck to remember Grandma.'

Raphael began to lift the sea-green elixir from around his neck.

'What are you doing?' Miri stopped him.

'Grandma said it was for you.'

Miri was puzzled. 'Keep it with you,' Miri insisted. 'I like that the two are together. I still cannot imagine she has been waiting all her life for the flower to make this elixir.

'What do you mean she believes the elixir is intended for me?' Miri laughed.

Raphael hesitated. He wanted to tell Miri everything Ava had said about the elixir and the monster.

'I am glad you caught up with me,' Miri interjected. The laughter had melted her face and softened her body. 'You must have walked about thirty-five kilometres every day!'

'Sometimes more, and into evening if the weather was cool.' Raphael smiled. 'I promised Grandma I would catch up to you. She said it was very important. She says your life is in danger. That I had to rush to reach you. What does it all mean, Miri? She speaks in riddles but she was so sure that something, or someone, means you harm and I must be close to protect you.'

'She said many things to us at breakfast, I remember.'

'But seeing you here, on the Camino. We are walking together. There is nothing here to harm us. Grandma's world of monsters does not make sense any more.'

Miri, too, felt safe on the Camino.

'It does not matter what she means, Raphael. I loved Ava's stories too. But she also told us that her stories, her knowledge of the flower, the elixir, they all held clues. Her stories were not meant to be taken literally. You and I will never know the true meaning of her foretelling. You and I have been part of her story, that is true. But we have completed our part. The elixir is now around your neck. And now, the story will continue with others. Look around. Let us enjoy what we have here. The Camino is so incredible.'

Raphael had to agree. 'Even Grandma was finding the meaning difficult to interpret, to explain,' he confessed.

'I do believe in Ava's gift. She taught me to see my angels for the first time. I did not even know I had angels. Raphael, they will warn me if something wants to harm me. There is so much I have to learn and understand. I do not want to think about Ava's monsters. I just want to speak with my angels, see my angels, and learn to see the world through my angels. Just like Ava. I am experiencing a new world, a new life.

'So stop worrying. Let us just enjoy our Camino, our Camino friends, each other.'

Raphael nodded, feeling better. 'Just accept the now.' He understood.

Miri shouted with joy. 'At last!'

Hari did not accept.

Hari wanted.

38

The Bridge

At each dawn waking, and with his head still on his pillow, the two elixir bottle always drew Raphael's gaze. He loved their shape, the angel-winged lids, and he loved the sharpness in the colours of the two liquids. And every morning he would inspect the colours. Always a subtle change which, he thought, only he noticed.

'They look different today.' Sara noticed too.

Raphael was surprised and pleased she noticed, because the reason he loved the bottles the most is that he remembered his grandma when he looked at them. And when Sara asked him what the bottles were, he was able to talk about his grandma.

'Tell me again about the two bottles, what's in them?' Sara felt like talking.

Raphael had not had his first café con leche yet. *Why not?* he thought. And he launched into the recipe and the making of the elixir. He must have bored Sara. Sara's expression of love towards two men cycling past drew out her truth.

'*Que culo,*' she shouted, followed with a loud laugh. And then, in honour of the particularly handsome young cyclist, she began a song and a dance. The shout drew her friends to join Sara's infectious laugh. For they all knew that Sara's truth was theirs too.

During a moment of quiet walking, Raphael shared with Carmen from Murcia his truth, that he had not loved before. He was scared of love. He did not think he knew what love was and was just beginning to learn the language of love. Carmen told how she had lived an empty marriage to a man who had believed he loved her, and whom she thought she loved. She described how the marriage drained her of her being.

'I stopped living. Just existing in that empty life. I forgot myself. I am learning to live again. I cannot remember what it feels like to be touched with love. His love was not the love I needed.' Carmen's words gave voice to the pain in her soul.

Miri was walking with Keitaro and she had been watching Raphael and Carmen walking together ahead of her. When she saw Keitaro's angel, and his attention to Carmen, she had to tease Carmen.

'Maybe love and passion has already discovered you. He is beautiful!'

Carmen turned around and laughed in infectious joy. Carmen's angel already knew.

Later, when Carmen and Keitaro began walking together and slowing their pace, and conveniently no one else was able to walk with them at their pace, everyone waited for their story to unfold.

'There is a saying in my guidebook…' Miri

wondered if Raphael would guess.

He looked at her blankly.

'The Camino brings you what you need, not what you want.'

Approaching the Roman bridge across the river in Hospital de Órbigo, Raphael was sensing a different kind of bridge.

'I feel like I am leaving something behind.'

'The Meseta?' Miri suggested. She was still missing the painted landscape.

'Do you feel your body moving differently? Like we are floating or sailing as we walk?' Raphael asked, trying to explore.

'Which is it? Floating or sailing?' Miri was glad to be distracted from her aching feet.

'Sailing. I cannot feel the ground any more, but my legs are moving, one in front of the other. I am moving forward. I am sailing.'

'Yours might be sailing; my feet are aching. But I cannot feel my mochila any more. There is no weight on my back. And these distances we are walking. We are no longer counting the distance, just walking. What will we walk today? Twenty-five, thirty, forty km? A few weeks ago, walking twenty kilometres was unthinkable. Absurd.'

Carmen, a history teacher, had been waiting for the bridge. 'A Spanish noble — you will love his name, Don Suero de Quiñones, fought ten knights for the love of one woman on this bridge.'

'How would you know a thing like that?' Sara tested. The longest Roman bridge in the world suddenly became even more irresistible.

'Hey Keitaro,' Sara added. 'Did you hear that? I think you need will need to fight for Carmen's hand.'

Carmen jumped, screamed and acknowledged the challenge.

'Yes, but did this Don something win her hand?' Keitaro called, genuinely intrigued.

'Of course he did!' Sara guessed, looking at Carmen for some support.

'Something called love!' Raphael tried to encourage.

'And passion,' Aurora added.

They all stopped in the middle of the bridge to admire the views and to take photographs.

'This is also the town where Don Quixote was taken sick and the doctors proclaimed him mad.'

'I feel I want to stay on the Camino forever. I do not want this journey to end,' Miri confessed.

Raphael and Keitaro, having walked the path the year before, glanced at each other with knowing smiles.

'I think I used the same words last year!' Raphael shared.

'Me too,' Keitaro admitted, still smiling. 'And probably just about here too.'

'The Camino is not finished with us,' offered Miri.

Just as they thought they were about to cross the waiting half of the bridge, Keitaro decided to accept

Sara's challenge and began a theatre. He raised his walking stick above him and held it high, as if it were a medieval weapon, a fighting pole. To add to the drama, he stood with his arms wide and his knees bent pretending to be a Japanese warrior.

'I make a challenge for the hand of the maiden!' Keitaro shouted. His intention clear.

'I will be the maiden!' Carmen was quick to volunteer.

'Who will fight me?' Keitaro was satisfied.

'She will be mine!' Raphael accepted the challenge.

Raphael and Keitaro faced one other. Ready for battle.

'Wait, Carmen needs a scarf.' Sara untied her red *pañuelo* and handed it to Carmen.

Carmen waved the red scarf above her head, and the duel began.

The two makeshift knights, on the longest bridge in the Roman and medieval world, enacted a fighting drama scene, complete with the live action slow motion, for the hand of the pilgrim maiden, Carmen.

The pilgrims shouted, clapped and encouraged them. As more pilgrims arrived, they too cheered, laughed, photographed and even videoed the two mochila-carrying slow-motion warriors.

Keitaro won, of course. And to great applause, he reached out and grabbed the scarf from Carmen's waiting hand.

Carmen was his.

39

Foncebadón

Tasting the chocolate of Astorga in front of Gaudi's Palace while watching Miri dance around the plaza was a moment, Raphael decided, he would not forget. If only he could collect moments and package them, he thought to himself.

'I know,' Raphael called out to Miri before Miri could say anything.

'Francisco of Assisi came here.'

Miri laughed and danced to the cathedral where she collected her blessing and *sello*, and then danced again until she reached the fountain of youth and miracles a short distance out of Astorga.

'Let's fill our bottles.' Miri emptied her bottle and began refilling it with the cold freshness of the healing fountain.

When two pilgrims walked passed without stopping, Miri was surprised.

'They did not see this fountain of youth?'

'They were talking about booking their flights from Santiago.' Raphael had watched them pass and heard their conversation.

'They are no longer on the Camino. Santiago is

arriving.' Miri did not dance the rest of the day.

The silent mood of reflection was only broken at the entrance of the albergue in Rabanal where, as they arrived, they witnessed an unusually stubborn voluntario arguing with a pilgrim, refusing her entry.

Keitaro tried to intervene.

'What's wrong?'

The pilgrim explained she had a back problem, was in a lot of pain.

'I arranged to have my mochila transported here. But the voluntario is not interested.'

'Go!' The voluntario raised his voice again at her. 'Only pilgrims who carry their mochila allowed.'

'Follow me,' said Keitaro, lifting her mochila. 'The albergue round the corner is much better than this one.'

'The Mountain of Burdens is approaching,' Miri said softly to the tearful woman.

The group, and everyone else who had witnessed the spectacle, stepped away from the voluntario and his albergue and followed Keitaro.

Keitaro was right. The albergue he led them to was not only better, more comfortable but welcoming to all. Instead of the usual bunk beds, the group of pilgrims slept on single beds that night. As the curfew lights went out, Keitaro remarked softly, 'There is a saying by an ancient poet, "Be grateful for what we do not receive".'

'Rumi, I think,' the woman Keitaro had rescued whispered.

I need to read Rumi, Miri decided.

Raphael touched Miri's arm gently, she was already awake. It was four-thirty a.m. Raphael was hoping to catch the sunrise in Foncebadón.

They walked silently together in the face-numbing cold mountain morning air, disturbing the feeding deer and watching the fading stars.

'I am happy to be here. With you.' Miri touched Raphael's hand.

Raphael did not reply.

When they reached Foncebadón, the sun had not yet risen. Raphael led Miri to a wall of an abandoned building. Dropping their rucksacks, they climbed the wall to a perfect viewpoint, an incredible panorama of hills, mountains and the sky. The beauty that began to unfurl in front of them was extraordinary. Raphael was glad to have woken early and to have made it in time.

The yellow ball rose over a distant mountain like an erupting fire. An orange painted crescendo coloured the sky. A few enquiring, unsuspecting small grey clouds found themselves gilded with bright golden edges, while an aeroplane caught the rising sun's reflection, and like a comet, marked its path across the sky. And finally, a ray of yellow orange dawn sunlight touched Raphael and Miri's bodies, leaving behind a new blessing in their hearts.

New words.

Neither could take their eyes away from the new words.

'I thought the Meseta was a painting. I am in

another world,' Miri breathed.

Raphael captured the image on his phone camera. 'That photo should be on the cover of a book,' Miri declared when Raphael shared it.

The light, not the sunrise, or the sun continued to enter Miri's soul. And Miri felt the word, the word that was missing in her diary.

'I caught this sunrise last year. I did not know if it would happen again but I had to try. Something told me to be here, to share this moment with you.' Raphael was thrilled and moved.

'Beauty hides pain,' said Miri, finding a taste of the word inside her.

'Pain hides beauty.' Raphael played with her as he captured a second image of the moment on his camera. 'In this one you look like you have wings, you look like an angel.' Raphael smiled. 'Let's have some Indian chai,' he suggested.

'Indian chai? Here? In this little village? On top of this mountain? With this perfect sunrise? Do not tease.'

Miri followed Raphael to the albergue which was immediately behind them.

'Not possible!' Miri sipped her Indian tea and understood she was still discovering the Camino.

'This is only the beginning. We are close to the Cruz de Ferro. The Mountain of Burdens.' Raphael remembered Amelia. 'Only a few kilometres away.'

Miri glimpsed the cross just above the tree line with still a kilometre to walk. But she had a question for her angel.

'I want to know what you see when you look at me,' Miri asked her angel.

'I do not know who you are. But I can show you what I see.'

Miri was still practising and learning to ask the right questions. But how does one prepare to talk with an angel?

'I want to see the world with my eyes and with your senses.'

The angel did not reply.

'I cannot see anything.' Miri was not convinced. 'Am I nothing?'

The angel did not reply.

And then Miri felt a pink light. Ahead was the Cruz de Ferro, but this light was not in front of her, it was inside her. Miri felt the light inside her.

'Thank you for showing me how you see me.'

But the angel was not finished. Miri knew she was being guided a little deeper. Her senses cleared a little more, like the morning mist.

Miri's heart caught something else inside the light, little stars she thought, something more than herself, and before she had even asked her angel, Miri realised instantly that the light was from her angel.

Again, the angel was not finished. The angel took her further, deeper again.

This other light is stronger than me, but not part of me. Miri thought it was blue. *I do not know what it is, why it is there. Is this the mystery I am not supposed to see or know?* The question was a thought; Miri did not need to speak to the angel. The angel was part of her.

The mystery has always been part of me, I understand. She had grown with the mystery. It had been with her all her life. She accepted it. But she had never been aware of it before. And before she could explore any more, a tall cross reaching into the sky and caressing a mound of small stones reached her eyes. A group of seven young pilgrims were holding hands and forming a chain around the Cruz de Ferro, while another of the group was standing in the middle and reciting a prayer.

There was silence.

The sound of footsteps, the prayer, the cross, the stones under the feet were so unexpected, Miri's music launched loudly inside her. Miri could not control it. Stepping into her soul, deeper into her rhythm, deeper then she could ever remember, she danced.

Even as she began her dance, Miri unclipped and dropped her mochila; she was an expert, now. Miri danced the past and, without knowing, danced her future. Her soul wrote the words of her life through her body so only those who knew the language of the universe would recognise the invisible sketches she painted with her footsteps.

Walking behind, Raphael picked up Miri's discarded mochila and dropped his with hers in an open grassy area before collapsing on the mochilas and lay there, facing the Cross of Burdens.

The silent and sometimes whispered movement of the pilgrims and the collection of hidden memories in the stones around the Cruz de Ferro overwhelmed him, as it had the previous year. Miri's dance engulfed the moment.

Raphael had to wipe away the tears from his face at least twice. Miri's dance was love. More than love. She was dancing memories, pain, she was dancing every stone, every burden on the mountain. He tried to find the words, but none came and none fitted. And so he watched and allowed his tears to feel.

'I am writing a dance with my heart and cannot see one word.' Miri confused Raphael as she danced around him before returning to the mound of burdens and memories.

I have no words to tell you that I love you, Raphael's heart spoke. And Miri saw Raphael's angel when she danced around him a second time.

The sun began to creep over the trees and brought with it a rising mist from the valley. Miri's movements came alive in the mist. To Raphael and anyone who saw her, she looked like a dream, maybe even an angel. To be sure, she looked as if she did not belong in this world. And there was one moment she was carrying, maybe leaving behind, that also did not belong in this world.

While Miri continued her dance, Raphael recovered from his tears to retrieve a small white stone, given to him by Amelia, from a little zippered pouch on the front of his mochila. He checked his phone messages to find the prayer she had sent him the night before, the prayer for the Mount of Burdens. Raphael carried his phone and the stone and climbed the mound, feeling every stone under his feet. At the cross he knelt. Raphael tried to touch the essence of Amelia's grief, but no one can feel the grief of a loved one left behind. Raphael invited and felt the presence of Amelia's husband. Had he followed Raphael? Had he walked the Camino too? And while reciting and recording the prayer, he laid Amelia's burden upon the other stones to rest for eternity. "Your prayers and burdens are now on the Camino, left behind at the Mountain of Burdens, and they will always be here on the Camino. Lots of love and thoughts, Raphael." Raphael pressed an arrow on the phone and sent the message and video recording to Amelia.

Amelia's tears did not stop that day as the video of her prayer and her stone being left at the Mount of Burdens was replayed countless times.

There was one more burden to leave behind. Raphael found the coin, the coin that he had collected from the Mountain of Forgiveness. He remembered his grandma.

'Take it to the Cruz de Ferro,' she had insisted after inspecting it. 'Carry the memory of me with this coin. The coin found you and I think this coin wants to be left at the Cruz de Ferro, Raphael. Tell Miri to leave her burdens at the Cruz. And remember me, my love.'

Raphael remembered the love that his grandma had

filled his life with. He thanked his grandma. He knelt again and let the coin drop from his fingers.

'I love you, Grandma. Thank you for loving me, never judging me, for teaching me to discover the love inside me.'

The Cruz de Ferro is an endless prayer. Miri was listening to the wind. And she wondered if she should pray. But she had no words for the moment, only feelings and sensations. So she danced and watched the silhouetted hopes of the arriving pilgrims, and she watched their gentle hands caress the love in their stones, and she watched their tears as they left behind their prayers, memories, burdens and sometimes, their grief. She watched the scene around the cross. Miri thought the mountain was alive too. She watched the mountain welcome all who approached, and embrace all the stones. An endless embrace that also gathered Miri's footprints. Footprints that climbed the stones to the cross where she felt the memories of loved ones who would never be left behind.

Some pilgrims took a photo, some read prayers, some sang a psalm, some wept, many wept.

'So young,' said Miri, reading one stone before she placed her small black stone with a thin white stripe across the middle next to a striking white stone which caught her eye. Leaning against the white stone was a bronze 1968 Spanish peseta. Miri instantly remembered the coin.

Miri did not dance after the Cruz de Ferro.

40

Silence

Miri did not dance after the Cruz de Ferro.

The dance was not a burden, so why had the dance in her body been left behind? she asked her angels.

The music was not a burden, why had the rhythm she had only recently rediscovered been left behind?

But the angels did not answer.

The steep descent into Acebo culminated in a prolonged café con leche stop with a now routine gentle massage of painful knees.

'Here or Ponferrada?' Raphael wondered out loud, relaxing into his coffee.

'Let's sleep with the Knights of the Castle,' Miri decided, reading her guidebook. The knees had recovered quickly.

No other words were needed for the remainder of the day or evening.

When Miri and Raphael looked at one another, they both already knew something new was happening to them, around them.

At the albergue in Ponferrada, Miri waited for the ghosts of the Knights Templar that watched over the pilgrims. But when she closed her eyes, she sunk into a deep, heavy slumber and missed the arrival of the knights.

The new hope that woke both Miri and Raphael also brought renewed energy. The words also returned.

'It seems like the Camino is taking us, guiding us,' said Raphael, with surprise. 'After all the aches and pains, we are almost flying!'

At a coffee shop in Cacabelos, Miri opened her guidebook and studied the profile of the remainder of the Camino.

'Looks like a difficult climb ahead.' But this time, there was something else on Miri's mind. 'The last mountain before Santiago.'

'Let's cross the mountain first!' Raphael cautioned, remembering the steep climb. 'A few days ago you told me to live in the now, to accept the now,' he teased.

Miri's hope flickered with the tease. 'I found the Mountain of Burdens very moving.' Miri had been waiting.

'Yes, I found it sad too.' Raphael was also ready to share. 'I feel a strange sense of relief that the mountain is behind me. As if the burdens had been weighing heavily.'

Raphael described his emotions when leaving behind Amelia's prayer and the coin for his grandma. 'Every moment was special. Watching pilgrims arriving and witnessing the act of their leaving behind a stone, a burden, was very touching.

'But when I was watching you dance, I felt my eyes water. I have seen you dance many times and each time

I have smiled, laughed with you, enjoyed your joy. But on the Mountain of Burdens, you were dancing my life, my pain, and the burdens of everyone around us. I was overwhelmed by your dance. How do you know my pain? How do you hear the lives? The burdens, the experiences? How do you turn them into your dance?'

Miri did not answer. She did not need to.

'Did you leave anything behind at the Mountain of Burdens?' Raphael asked.

Miri only smiled her reply. She did not know how to reply.

Raphael understood. He knew she would reply when he was ready to understand.

The long stretch of walk along the highway into Vega followed by the steep climb through the misty, drizzly, cold mountain rain towards O Cebreiro made Miri tetchy.

'I want a hot drink right now.' Miri stopped to complain at the damp clouds surrounding them and when the steep climb refused to cease. 'I bet these mountain people have never seen the sun!'

Raphael laughed. 'Don't stop,' he shouted, passing Miri. 'Next coffee shop is not far; I will buy you every hot drink they have! Come on,' he encouraged.

'I have a photograph of the sun on my phone. I will show it to the next farmer we pass!' Miri threatened.

'You will have to call an ambulance too, you will scare him. The farmer will not know what it is, he will have a heart attack.'

The banter led to the first coffee shop and also to the first Tarta de Santiago. The taste of the cake suddenly made the steep climb, cloudy panorama and the cold drizzle bearable.

'Does this Tarta mean we are in Galicia?' Miri asked.

The answer arrived on a steep stretch of the mountain with the Galicia stone marker. Raphael was hesitant to take a photo. Galicia was the last province of the Camino. He wondered what would happen to the two of them after Santiago. He did not want the Camino to end.

A little too quickly, the steep climb was replaced by the stone echoes between the narrow streets of O Cebreiro. The cobbled streets buzzed with rushed voices, howling winds and flying waterproof layers. Each pilgrim was eager to find a little warmth and shelter in one of the many bars.

Instead of the bar, Raphael led Miri into the church of San Francisco.

'There is a tale of the holy grail being hidden here,' Raphael whispered, as they joined the ongoing mass.

'Only a tale?' Miri's hope was still strong.

The drizzle did not stop the next day, but the Camino friends had found each other again in the Albergue Municipal in O Cebreiro, and the joy of walking together made the descent into Triacastela almost festive.

In Triacastela, while their friends searched for a

bed, Miri had an idea.

'An albergue called El Beso is in the next village.' Miri looked at Raphael.

Raphael, a little wet and bothered, smiled at the name and checked the distance in Miri's guidebook: two km. He insisted on a coffee before continuing.

El Beso welcomed the pilgrims with a kiss. Miri and Raphael both laughed at their fortune when they entered the dormitory and found that that the two central bunks at the top of a wooden bed cathedral, a cacophony of Camino art almost touching the roof, were still vacant.

After the communal meal of forest-harvested nettle soup and wild vegetables, the forest-grown wooden bunk beds called everyone to sleep and the beds filled quickly.

'I want a kiss,' demanded Miri.

Nothing will ever be as beautiful as Camino love, Raphael thought. He held her close. He was glad to be in El Beso, at the top of the tower, holding Miri.

Miri needed the closeness.

'Something is watching me. I am very aware of it. I feel it,' she whispered, now relaxing a bit.

Raphael held her gently, stroking her back, her skin, her hair. He knew something had been troubling her.

'I felt a change after the Mountain of Burdens. We were both unsettled. I wondered why you stopped dancing after the Cruz de Ferro.'

Miri nodded. 'Last night, in my sleep, in O Cebreiro, I felt something approach. When I woke I thought I had been dreaming, but I have not dreamt since Ava's, and then I realised it was not a dream, it left behind its intention, Raphael. It was watching me.'

Raphael paused.

'What did you feel? Did you find the monster? Or did the monster find you?'

Miri snuggled closer, she enjoyed feeling Raphael's heartbeat over hers.

'Ava told us she saw something in the dream we shared. That something was waiting for me. I was dismissive. I want to understand. Tell me again, tell me everything she told you after I left.'

It was Miri's turn to listen.

Raphael repeated what happened the morning when Miri left, but with more detail, as much as he could remember.

'She did not know what this monster is, and I do not want you fighting any monsters, Miri. As you already said, her words, her foretelling, they are metaphors, stories, emotions, suggestions, clues. I love my grandma, but she has always spoken in riddles.'

Miri was not convinced and remained unsettled.

'One more thing, Raphael.' Miri explained how Ava had taught her to speak with her angel and described how she had seen her angel in León.

Raphael was not surprised, he had grown up with Ava and her mystery. Raphael was happy for Miri. And listening about Miri's world was like listening to Ava. He did not need to ask questions or seek explanations. Listening to flowers was enough for him. He wondered if he might ever see an angel.

'But since the Mountain of Burdens, Raphael, I have not been able to speak to my angels. I sense their presence; Ava taught me how to feel them. But they are not with me, they are distracted, looking elsewhere, at something or someone. Last night, I felt a small feeling of what they are looking at. Whatever my angels are seeing, if it is important, I must learn to see it too. I have only just been introduced to my angels, I cannot lose them.'

Raphael thought for a moment; the solution was clear.

'Walk on your own tomorrow,' he said, holding her closer. 'Practise what my grandma taught you. Do the meditations as you walk.'

Raphael wondered how Miri had come into his life. He felt grateful to the universe for Miri.

'Aurora walks alone every day, and we always meet up in the evening. We can do the same.'

Miri agreed, feeling better.

'Barbadelo,' Raphael gave her instructions before they closed their eyes. 'Walk through Sarria tomorrow. Barbadelo is the next village. I will meet you at the first albergue there.'

Even when pilgrims walk together, souls walk alone.

41

The Tunnel

Miri's angels did not reply through Sarria. In Barbadelo, where the albergue had a swimming pool, Miri spent the evening hiding her unease by sunbathing, swimming and laughing with her Camino friends. If Miri sensed their presence again in the night, it was only a passing thought.

In Portomarin, where Miri looked down from the bridge and saw the old town submerged in the river, she asked her angels to look with her, the angels did not answer. Miri did not enter the new town. In Gonzar, where she battled cows and flies for one more café con leche, Miri sensed her angels, but nothing more. *They are slipping away from me*, she thought.

At the *Pulpería* in Melide, where the friends met together to share the delicacy of the town with a bottle of cola, Miri was quiet.

'You remind me of my grandmother, Miri.' Raphael made an attempt to involve Miri. 'The way you look at the food.'

Raphael looked up and saw a sweet smile on Miri's face, as he had intended.

'I never knew my grandma could see angels. Even

though she is blind, she used to look at me the same way as you are now.'

'I have had better octopus,' Miri complained.

'It's true,' agreed Aurora.

Miri was waking extra early each morning. Always the first to leave the albergue. And every morning, to her surprise, she always came across the same silent family, a tall, thin teenager with her parents. And every morning, she made sure to avert her gaze from their angels, she only wanted to see her own. That she had never seen or heard the family speak to one another, was always her first thought. Her second was that she recognised the family from the train to St Jean Pied de Port.

Each time she passed the silent family, Miri's memory took her back to St Jean Pied de Port. The daily impossible distances listed in the guidebook. The disbelief and shock that she could walk over the mountain to Roncesvalles. She even remembered the signpost on the road out of Roncesvalles, did it say 780 km? And yet, here she was, with only 50 km left to walk. The entire journey, the distances she had covered, felt unreal. But the distances covered each day were real. And she was real. The rucksack had lost all its weight, her boots had stopped touching the ground, and she was sure, like Raphael, that she was flying when she walked.

Miri could not remember feeling so healthy and strong. The stress in her neck and shoulders she had carried to St Jean Pied de Port was no more. And when she entered her deeper sensations and feelings, in particular how she felt about Raphael, she remembered his embrace in El Beso, and she was embarrassed. She could not help but compare the difference in his touch to that of her last lover. While the grief inside her heartbreak remained as a scar, the anger and sadness of grief was no more. But she also understood that it was not Raphael, but the heartbreak had brought her to the Camino. Miri even wondered if she should be grateful to the heartbreak, and the two words on Facebook.

The Bull with four horns, her protector, did not know love or heartbreak. And while the Bull caught a glimpse of the distraction, the reason he had brought Miri to the Camino, he trusted the Camino. There was nothing more to do. Nothing he could do. Even protectors cannot know every thread of the universe. And fate was a very thin, almost unseen, thread.

One morning, coming out of Arzúa, Miri passed the silent family once more. She admired their silence, but today she decided to see their angels. Their angels caught her gaze. Each was struggling to find love, to know love, Miri understood. And while no words passed between the pilgrims, Miri comforted their angels. 'I did not know that living love can change a person, a life, so much.'

It may have been too early in the morning for the angels to reply.

Raphael was always on her mind. And when Miri remembered that Raphael could not see himself, could not see his reflection, Miri understood that it was not her soul that had achieved the feat of the walk along the Camino. It was not her mind, for had she only trusted her mind, within the first five km from St Jean Pied de Port, she would have surrendered and taken a train to a beach resort in the south of Spain.

Her body had never once complained or given up. Sure there were aches and pains and blisters and even a few bruises. Sure there was the shock of sharing toilets, bathrooms and sometimes even beds. The discomfort of walking in rain, and often the intense heat under the sun. While her mind had done so, her body never complained or demanded to turn back.

She sensed her body and loved her body, as if she were sensing it for the first time.

All this time, all her life, she had looked in the mirror, she had seen her reflection, but she had forgotten the magic of life that lived inside her body, her being. And she thought she understood Raphael a little more.

Her body was the reason she felt so good, so strong, so complete, so connected, so free. And her body had walked despite her mind's protestations. Her body had carried her soul along the Camino, all these kilometres. Her body had carried her soul all her life. Her body felt love. Her body felt Raphael's touch. Her body was the real magic.

'The final ingredient for life.' The voice came from her angels.

'Where have you been?' Miri asked.

There was no reply.

And if Miri thought the angels would bring her comfort again, only the thought of Raphael returned her to the comfort she wanted.

Approaching an empty bench under the shade of a tree by a small stream, Miri decided to stop and feel her angels.

'Without your body, we cannot experience love,' the voices began again. 'Without your body, your soul could not experience this Camino.'

'So life is not my soul. Life is my body which carries my soul?' Miri tried, thinking she had understood.

'Without our body, we would not know love,' the angels repeated.

And with that reply, her soul caught the sensation of a whisper. Seven whispers. And the universe sang for Miri. The seven voices composed a celebration, for the seven voices only recognised love.

And today they recognised Miri.

Miri's body wept at the sound of the seven voices.

Miri's soul knew her time to return to the realm of spirits had come.

When Miri stood again and her soul did not let go of the song of the whispers, she wiped her face, and allowed her body to take the comfort in the embrace of the mochila one last time. She allowed her eyes to follow the arrows and lead her body to her moment. And so, when she arrived at the tunnel of Garim, when she saw the monster, she was not surprised. She was not scared.

She knew.

For every living being, there is a moment, a time to pass, a time to die. This moment was her time.

Miri had one regret.

'I wish I had loved more,' she said, as if confessing to her angels. 'My time without angels, without seeing love, was nothing,' she said to her soul and her body and to her angels. 'I wish I had created more time to love, and be loved.'

'Time is only created by those who have forgotten love,' the whispers answered.

42

Death

At the riverside Albergue Municipal in Ribadiso da Baixo, by the open window that faced the flowing river, Raphael could not sleep or greet the restless night.

Raphael had checked for Miri in the two village albergues the evening before, she was not listed in either. She had not received his messages and he was too tired to walk on.

Raphael blamed the heat of the night for keeping him awake. For a while he blamed the loud rush of the river. But he chose not to blame the new sensations he was feeling for Miri. A glance at his phone: 4.04 a.m. Raphael used the moment to escape from his bed, and his thoughts.

Stepping into the cold darkness of the damp early morning, Raphael climbed a short hill, crossed the highway, and continued on through the built-up suburbs towards the lights of Arzúa. He wondered if Miri was ahead. But there was no movement, no silhouettes, and it was too early for shadows.

Raphael walked at his deliberate early morning pace. He knew a good coffee shop in Arzúa. By the time he reached it, the small café was open and already full of locals heading to work and a handful of pilgrims enjoying the magical waking of a café con leche and a freshly baked warm croissant.

Raphael did not expect to see Miri, but his eyes did not tire looking for her.

This café held a memory from Raphael's previous Camino. Wandering through the town, he was desperate for his first café con leche but all the bars were closed. Just as he was about to give up, he happened across a Danish pilgrim and her mother.

'Follow us,' the pilgrims invited.

The bar was slightly off the Camino. The pilgrims had sat together on the corner table. Raphael sat at the same table and remembered the moment. He knew he needed to remember. Few pilgrims talk in the morning. But something had made Raphael voice three early words.

'You woke early.'

The younger pilgrim, without hesitation, shared her tragedy, one that Raphael was deeply affected by and one that would remain with him forever. The pilgrim was walking her grief in memory of her three children. One, no more than a few months old. All killed in an unspeakable crime. Raphael asked the names of the three children; he already knew that for as long as he could walk, he would walk one Camino in memory of each child.

He remembered the children. His second Camino. He already knew he would return the next year. He

271

wondered if his Camino would carry and hold the memory of the children. And he also wondered if the wish, the dedication, was a selfish one. A feeling for the loss of a child he never had.

Regenerated by the café con leche, or maybe the fresh chocolate croissant, Raphael returned to the street. Just as he was about to turn into the Camino again, he noticed a pilgrim walking ahead, away from the yellow arrow. He called to her. When she turned, he pointed the way. She was grateful. Raphael waited for her to make sure, and as she drew closer, Raphael recognised her.

'I hope I did not wake you this morning,' Raphael said apologetically. The lady had been sleeping in the bunk below.

The two walked together through the forests after Arzúa, telling each other stories from their lives.

'I am sixty-eight years old; I have travelled from the US. I think I have one more Camino left in me. I will walk again next year if my niece wants to come.'

'You are too young to stop walking Caminos,' Raphael said encouragingly. 'The oldest pilgrim I walked with last year was a seventy-seven-year-old lady from Canada. And this year, I met a pilgrim from Spain who is eighty-two!'

They appreciated each other's company, conversation and pace.

'Shall I slow down?' Raphael offered, a little concerned.

'This is the fastest I have walked along the Camino

and I am so enjoying it. Do not slow down, I am glad to be walking with you.'

Raphael's companion was thrilled with her pace.

They watched the sunrise through the trees, the mist lift over the valley, and only parted when the lady stopped at a bar.

'My bag will be arriving at the next albergue so I will slow down now,' the pilgrim explained, grateful to Raphael.

Raphael did not remember the rest of that day. He did not know how far he walked. But he would always remember the next moment. The moment he walked into a tunnel.

Tunnels are dark.

Raphael's eyes adjusted to see two pilgrims kneeling. Not kneeling: the two pilgrims had dropped their mochilas and were attending to someone. Voices. *Ambulance*, the only word he heard. One more step and he recognised a third discarded mochila. A wave of shock and terror ran through Raphael's body.

43

The Monster

'I know you.' Miri recognised the eyes.

The Bull stared at Miri. Even Hercules and Gilgamesh had shown fear in the face of the creature.

The Bull saw the goodness in front of him, it could not take its eyes away from the goodness.

'I know your eyes. Like I have seen you in the heavens, in the stars, in my dreams.' There was a presence in the eyes that Miri recognised.

Miri was not afraid. She may have been a little surprised that she was not afraid.

Miri paused and corrected her thoughts. Not the heavens or the stars or her dreams. Her angel. Her angel had recognised the creature.

The Bull was ready to strike the fatal blow. But the Bull did not move. The words held the creature with an unexpected pause.

No challenger had ever spoken to the Bull at the start of a battle before. The creature fought with weapons, not words. What were the purpose of these words? He had no words to return. Only weapons of destruction.

'I have seen you before.' Miri repeated after

noticing the hesitation. And this time more deliberately. 'You are a collector,' she persisted. 'But you do not collect.'

The Bull was only there to do battle. But why was this adversary covered in so much goodness?

'I can read you,' Miri continued. Miri was startled that the creature had an angel. 'You do not collect, you capture. You capture evil and take it far away.'

Miri's words had a strange effect. The words calmed the body of the Bull. This adversary knew the Bull. Knew the Bull's purpose. Every being had a purpose. What was this being's purpose?

Miri felt the change in the Bull. The questions, the Bull was intrigued with her words.

Yes, the Bull thought. *I battle with and capture evil, that is my purpose. But there is no evil here.*

The Bull had never been called to battle goodness before. And the goodness it saw in Miri mesmerised the Bull. The Bull saw a force — was it a healing? What was this force behind the goodness?

Evil was always terrified, petrified in the face of the creature. In Miri there was no fear. No terror.

The Bull wanted to know goodness and healing. The Bull remembered his youth. A time before the creature stepped into his life as warrior. The Bull remembered being given his purpose, to defeat evil and imprison it in the seventh firmament, far from life, far from Earth.

I am tired of battles and death and evil. The Bull

heard his own thoughts, and he had not thought for a long time. *I have forgotten what goodness and healing feels like.*

The Bull continued to stare at Miri. As with every creature of the heavens, the Bull did not see the body that Miri inhabited. The Bull saw her soul, her being, and the creature could not take his eyes away from the force that surrounded her.

'You want to know what goodness feels like?' Miri asked, reading his eyes and his angel. 'You have forgotten goodness.' Miri's voice did not confess to the surprise of the words that passed her lips.

She would not have been able to see, or read the Bull through her angel had Ava not taught her.

Miri dropped her rucksack. She calmly accepted the moment, sat down on the earth, and invited the Bull to sit opposite her. In return, she said, she would describe goodness. She would bring back the memories of the good the Bull had once felt in his life.

Miri described Raphael, her Amma and Appa, the Flower Collector. She described her hearts and the angels of love she saw.

She described her birth, her childhood and the love she received. And she described the love in the life around her, and the love showered on her by her new friends on the Camino.

'You are here to collect me.' She looked at the Bull. 'And since you have been summoned to collect me, you cannot leave without completing your task. You will collect my heartbeats.'

The Bull did not reply and Miri's eyes did not leave the Bull's presence and the face of his angel.

'I will give my hearts to you, freely,' Miri offered. 'But you must ask me for my hearts. If you ask me, I will forfeit all that I am, including my life, so that you can feel goodness again.'

This was no battle. This was a sacrifice. The Bull only knew battles, charges, strikes and blows. The Bull was a warrior who escorted heinous evil away from the world to a place seven ages away, seven universes away; some called the place the underworld and others, hell.

The Bull did not know choice, did not know how to ask, how to answer. The Bull only knew how to take.

To the Bull's surprise, Miri continued. 'Before you ask me for my hearts, before I give you my hearts freely, I have to hear your heart. I have to know what you will do with the goodness you will take from me. Where will you take it?'

The Bull said nothing.

The Bull only knew one place to take the collected. And goodness did not belong in the underworld.

Miri understood the confusion. 'But you must have my heartbeats. You must complete your task. And I must know what you will do with the goodness.'

The Bull and Miri were not alone.

Hari could not see the Camino, but Hari could see the Bull and Hari could see Miri. Hari was watching. Hari had never waited before.

Nothing is known in the universe. And nothing is unknown.

The Monster would take Miri away. Away from the force of the Camino that protected her. Hari would take the force from Miri. Hari would know the secrets of life, the secret of love. The secrets of something called time.

But then, Hari sensed the change in the creature.

So did Miri.

For the first time, the Bull did not want to take Miri.

'No,' said Miri. 'You have to complete your task. If you do not complete your task, you will cease to be. You will cease to have a purpose. You will cease to exist.'

The Bull knew the truth. Knew the consequence.

'You cannot die for me.' Miri understood the creature's fate.

And in that moment, one the creature would never forget, Miri's four hearts heard one another, and also understood that there was only one way a great mistake could be prevented.

'You must not die for me,' the Bull said to Miri. His first and last words.

But it was too late. The four hearts stopped, all at once, completing an act of selflessness, and taking away the very essence that violence could not understand and yet desired to know and feel: goodness. It was an instant. A moment, and Miri's body lay lifeless on the floor of the tunnel.

The creature stood in shock and stepped away from

Miri. It was not a feeling, it was a reflex. He was a warrior, was this a trap? The Bull felt nothing. Like all battles, the creature gained nothing and lost nothing.

But Miri had sacrificed herself to save the creature. And so the Bull was confused. The Bull had never known sacrifice before.

Nothing is known in the universe. And nothing is unknown.

And sacrifices are always unexpected.

'I was not living before I found you,' Raphael sobbed. 'Don't let me die a second time.'

But Miri was not listening.

Miri's life force was bleeding away.

44

Voices

Miri felt Raphael's arms, his touch, his kiss. She had never been held so close, with so much love, before. She wanted the moment to last, to feel more. She did not need to see his angel to know him, to know his love.

If she knew her life was ebbing away, Miri's face felt Raphael's tears. She chose not to remember her life, but chose to remain inside this moment of tenderness.

She did not hear the voices.

'Can I help? I am a doctor.'

'There is a pulse, it is weak. She is breathing. What happened?'

'This pulse. I have heard this rhythm before. This is not one heart. Her heartbeats are stopping, she is crashing. We need the ambulance.'

The Bull stood and watched from the end of the tunnel.

The Bull felt nothing.

In that instant, a body had fallen. Goodness was erased, exactly as the Bull had been tasked. But the Bull had stepped away before completing his task. The Bull had not carried the body away.

The moment had been interrupted.

The Camino is ready for every moment.

The Bull watched as his prey was being held by love. A force that would protect Miri, would not release Miri. The Bull could only look once more before disappearing, having gained nothing and lost nothing.

'I know this pulse. I know this rhythm. It is not possible.'

'The ambulance is here.'

'What is her name?'

'Miri.'

'I have lost her heartbeat.'

'I know this patient. Put the defibrillator away; her hearts will not understand. She has more than one heart. The machine will kill her. Put her in the ambulance. Connect her to the cardiac monitor. I need to see her readings.

'Quickly. I will talk you through what to do.

'Follow my instructions, she will live. I know what to do.'

The voices, the panic, the consequence of her heartbeats stopping, one by one, dawned on Miri. Miri's eyes were closed and yet she saw a deep pink light inviting her. Miri paused.

But Miri could not feel Raphael's arms any more.

And as she felt her life force leak away, the final thought on her skin was Raphael's touch.

And the final thought in her mind was his voice.

'Come back. Please come back.'

45

The Ambulance

'I remember you. Coming down the mountain after Pamplona. A long time ago. Your name? You are the café con leche pilgrim from Puente la Reina?'

'Raphael. I will call a cab and follow. What's the name of the hospital?'

'I am going with her to the hospital, Raphael. I will look after her. I am a doctor; I know her.'

Raphael was not listening.

'One of the hearts is beating, very faint, you were right,' the medic in the ambulance shouted.

'Good,' the doctor replied. 'I am coming.'

'I must go with her,' Raphael was panicking.

'No room in the ambulance. Listen to me. I know what to do. She will heal.' The doctor took out his phone. 'Dial your number, quick.'

Raphael took the phone from the doctor.

'Hurry, we have to move.'

Raphael dialled his own number, pressed the green button and returned the phone.

'Come back. Please come back,' Raphael sobbed, hoping Miri would hear, touching her hand and letting go.

The ambulance doors closed and began to moved away.

Raphael's phone rang.

46

The Surgeon

'Come back. Please come back.'

The surgeon remembered his final words to his late wife.

Being left behind, his heart was broken.

A surgeon who once fixed broken hearts. He did not want to be left behind.

A year after her passing, sitting in his lonely armchair in his quiet and lonely home, he waited for his time.

When, at the end of the year, his children collected their mother's clothes and jewellery and he saw the items in the charity shops, he understood he did not need to wait any longer. What happened to all the long walks and mountain treks they had planned together?

After his wife's stroke, they abandoned their plans and found new pleasures. They both feasted on each other's company, endless café con leche, Cola Cao, and pre-recorded TV dramas and documentaries.

Life changes in an instant. And he enjoyed his retirement because of her. She lived because of him. They might have been the sweetest years of their life together. Not needing to go anywhere. Just being together.

But the twenty-five years had taken their toll too. Caring for her, full time.

The twenty-five years troubled the surgeon.

He could not remember his before.

And then, by chance, although the surgeon already knew that chance was not a random or unexpected ornament, he was invited to say a few words at the opening of a new wing at his old hospital.

'You gave us my beautiful family,' Miri's mother whispered in his ear as she embraced him at the hospital reception, refusing to let him go. 'Did you ever take that walk? Did you ever meet the saint in the cathedral along the road that leads to the end of the world?'

When he tried to tell his children about the Camino, they were horrified.

'At your age? You will die! You will never return. You are not thinking about us!' his daughter protested.

The next morning, he closed his front door, posted his keys in the letter box, and walked to his local sports shop with his debit card.

'The Camino?' the young shopkeeper checked, raising his eyebrows.

The surgeon left his old clothes and shoes in the changing room.

'Please give them away,' he asked. 'I have a promise I must keep.'

With a pair of Camino shoes, blister-free socks, two strong walking sticks and a small rucksack containing what the shopkeeper called the essentials, his next stop was the train station.

He felt aggrieved that he could not say goodbye to his family. That they could not hear him. But his grievance did not last long, only until Pamplona where the train stopped and his Camino began.

He was walking a promise, made to the newborn's mother twenty-five years ago.

47

Time

Hari could not approach the Camino. He could not see the Camino. But he saw Miri. He would wait for the Bull to take the body away from the Camino.

And Hari watched and waited. Hari waited. Time had no meaning for Hari. And yet he waited. The waiting confused him.

Miri did not leave the Camino.

The Bull did not leave the Camino.

And when the Collector of Life did not arrive, Hari continued to wait.

And so in this moment, when Miri's hearts stopped, the waiting caused the world of the living to pause.

Every life Miri had touched, everyone who had seen her dance, even the man in the coffee shop who had watched her dance and called her a demon, paused.

It was as if time stood still, but it was only one heartbeat.

But for Miri's four hearts, the heartbeats numbered four. One for each heart.

And so the universe looked. And it looked four times. The universe looked at her birth, looked at her death, looked at her future, and looked at the Mountain of Burdens.

The world of spirits sensed a new feeling.

The world of demons sensed a long lost feeling.

The world of angels felt a force that they understood might be life, or could it be love?

And when the world of the living gained a heartbeat, those who looked within that heartbeat saw their future, others recollected their past, some dreamt an epic tale of rebirth, and there were also many who saw nothing, felt nothing, dreamt nothing.

In that same moment Hari, too, felt a pause. And his pause was a loss. Hari could no longer see the mystery. In fact, Miri disappeared completely. And in that same moment, Hari felt a new sensation. And he did not know what it was, so he discarded it, left it behind inside another moment. A moment he would never return to or find again, even when he learnt what it was.

Hari looked towards the universe for a consequence of the moment. But there was nothing there to read.

He needed. And he had not needed before. He still wanted.

The wanting continued to confused him.

And when the Collector of Life still did not arrive. He understood. Miri had not passed. Her soul was still connected to her body.

And the understanding surprised him.

This was not the moment for Miri's passing, he was waiting in the wrong moment.

And Hari was still learning about time.

The moment confused him.

The mystery was no more.

Miri was no more.

And Hari did not understand time. But he did understand being alone.

48

Santiago

Raphael's instinct battled to call a cab and follow the ambulance. Shock, disbelief and bewilderment left him unable to decide.

'The doctor is right.' A teary-eyed Carmen came to his rescue. 'We cannot help her. She is in the best of care, now. You heard what he said, her hearts will heal. Let them treat her.'

'The Camino is where she would want us to be, Raphael,' Keitaro also tried. 'If we walk, she will feel our Camino energy.'

Raphael was not convinced. 'She would want me to be there when she wakes.' He continued the battle.

'Waiting in a hospital room? Or walking the Camino?' Sara threw Raphael the challenge with a cheeky laugh and then a suggestion. 'Let's walk. You have the doctor's number. Right now, there is nothing you can do.'

'Once we have news that she is awake and well enough, we can all go to the hospital,' Aurora added.

Raphael was satisfied. Camino friends, Camino family.

The eucalyptus forests, the yellow arrows, the pilgrims, the friends… everything looked so normal, but the Camino did not feel real any more. Raphael remembered Ava's warnings about a monster. He felt guilty that he had been dismissive of her words. He wondered if he would share his fears with the group, but the words in his head made no sense to him. His words would make no sense to the group either, he decided.

'There is a new light in the air.' Keitaro's voice caught the pink rays through the eucalyptus trees. Some pilgrims even checked their smartphones to see if an eclipse was occurring.

Pink! Raphael remembered. He felt for the bottles around his neck. There was only one.

Raphael smiled his memory.

The path was silent until their feet tired and the Camino friends found a bar. Over a longer than usual café con leche break, Raphael decided to remember Miri and Ava with his friends.

'It was as if the two already knew each other and I was the stranger.' Raphael was describing Miri's meeting with Ava and Ava's art as a flower collector.

'That liquid around your neck, you made it with your grandmother from a flower?' Carmen was amazed at Raphael's skill.

'It is an elixir.' Raphael felt like a flower collector for the first time.

'I thought you had two bottles this morning,' Carmen observed.

Raphael's hand sprung to his neck, again, enjoying the pink memory before describing Miri's meeting with the flower. He kept his friends captivated all the way to Monte do Gozo by the tale of a flower that grew on the grave of an angel.

'What happened to the bottle?' Aurora tried to understand.

The silent queue at the albergue in Monte do Gozo tested Raphael's patience. As soon as he received his slip with his room and bed number, he rushed to take claim. The fresh silence of the empty room helped prepare him while he unpacked his phone and selected the last missed call.

The ring was immediately answered.

'Raphael? I am with her now. Her hearts are stable. She is breathing normally; she is awake.'

The words were enough to bring tears of relief to Raphael's exhausted eyes and he collapsed on his lower bunk. When his friends entered the room and saw the tears, they feared the worst.

'Thank you,' Raphael finished. 'Yes, they are listening.'

Raphael put his phone on speakerphone.

'Her heart is beating more steadily than ever before. To a former surgeon, like me, it sounds like she has received a new heart.' The surgeon coughed. 'She is recovering well.'

The surgeon heard the cheer.

'What happened to her?' Raphael asked.

'Well, that is a very complicated question, Raphael. The doctors, here, say it was a heart attack, not unlike the one I saw in her when she was born. I think I mentioned? I was the surgeon who repaired her hearts the day she was born.'

Raphael did not remember. His memory of the tunnel was a mess. His eyes widened at the realisation. A murmur of disbelief rounded the room.

'You are her surgeon? You were there, when she was born?' Raphael tried not to raise his voice. 'Are you joking with us?'

The surgeon chose not to answer. He was still struggling to understand.

'The doctors in this hospital did not believe me either. I had to introduce myself to the experts here and refer them to my research papers where I explained her case so they would allow me to work with them.

'Miri's hearts — she has four, did she tell you? — began to shut down, one by one. One young surgeon here, in the hospital, was convinced the hearts were damaged and Miri needed immediate surgery. But I had to slow them down. I knew what to do. Her hearts were in chaos. I had watched the struggle before, at her birth. I made them wait.

'Just as I had seen when she was a newborn, and as I expected, one heart at a time, the heartbeats began again. What I did not expect, is that the heartbeats slowly began to merge. The youngsters, the trainees had their own language. They described it as a reboot! They

293

have not seen anything like it. None of us have. Miri now has one heartbeat instead of four. Her breathing is normal. The nurses and doctors taking care of her, when I told them she was a pilgrim, have called her recovery a Camino miracle. They are already lighting candles to Santiago in the hospital chapel and speaking to journalists and priests,' he laughed.

Raphael could not say a word. His face was wet. His throat dry. Relief for Miri, and also himself. He wanted to hold her again. Is relief so selfish, he wondered?

'Maybe they are right, maybe it is a miracle,' the surgeon said softly, almost to himself. 'As if a fifth heartbeat has been waiting to wake inside her all this time, since she was born. This fifth heart has been waiting for her four hearts to stop, so that it could breathe life into her body today. The silent heart began beating today. I do not know anything about miracles; I do not know if this counts as one.'

A silent heart? Raphael's hand returned to the missing bottle around his neck. Raphael's eyes welled up remembering the elixir, remembering Ava, remembering the generation of flower collectors. He remembered words from Ava's stories: "The flower has a name, it is called the silent heart. It is the flower that will make the elixir for the silent heart."

Raphael questioned himself, his beliefs. Did he believe in the elixir? Of course he did! Why else would he have helped his grandmother prepare it; why else would he have carried it? And he could not help but wonder if Ava's foretelling, stories and preparations had saved Miri's life, and it was a pleasant thought. But Ava would not have encouraged the thought. The universe is more complicated than one elixir, she would have said.

'Before you ask…' The surgeon seemed to know what Raphael would ask. 'We are waiting for two more test results. I want to know what has happened to the four heartbeats. Miri's body has experienced a trauma and she is being prepared for two more scans to make sure her new heartbeat does not fall into chaos again, and also, the surgeons are trying to understand the cause. After the scans, her body will need to sleep and rest. So you will not be able to see her tonight, but she wants to see you all tomorrow.'

Relief overtook any disappointment.

'Now tell me, what was that pink liquid, from the bottle around your neck, that you sprinkled on her face and touched her lips with?'

Raphael remembered and paused. 'I cannot begin to thank you. I am wordless. You have not even told us your name.'

'Thank you!' the whole room shouted.

'Whatever brought you to the tunnel at the exact moment of Miri's need, my grandmother would have had an answer, but I do not.' Raphael was desperately trying to comprehend, even accept. 'You were there at Miri's birth?' he repeated. 'You are her heart surgeon?'

The surgeon laughed.

'This Camino is too much! May every force in the universe bless you.'

The surgeon acknowledge the gratitude. 'You have not answered my question.'

'The bottle contained nothing more than a flower elixir my grandmother made for Miri,' Raphael understated his explanation. 'Only natural oils and the essence of a very special flower Miri found along the Camino, collected and carried with her.' Raphael remembered the moment. 'And lots of love!' he added enthusiastically. 'I will tell you more when we meet. But I remember nothing that happened in the tunnel.' A partial truth. The only part of the moment in the tunnel Raphael recalled was a pink light and the voice of the elixir. Through his tears and emotions, a sound, not unlike the whisper of the flower, had caught him, and invited him to follow. Raphael knew he was following the elixir. He sensed the moment, followed the light, and known what to do, just as his grandmother had said.

'I only remember the panic and my emotions overflowing,' Raphael confessed.

'Mmm.' The surgeon paused. 'While you were holding her, and I was taking her pulse, I noticed a little bottle around your neck glow a beautiful, deep pink colour. The tunnel was dark so the glow caught my eye. The colour reminded me of the fuchsia my wife used to grow. I saw your eyes catch the glow too, as if you were conversing with it. You pulled the bottle from your neck, sprinkled the drops on her face, and let the final drops rest on her lips. Her skin seemed to breathe in the drops as they fell.'

Raphael listened. 'Miracles happen on the Camino.' It was Raphael's turn to be an expert.

The doctor chuckled. 'I believe you, Raphael. I only asked because two drops landed on my arm too, I still had my hand on her pulse when the drops fell on my skin… the oddest feeling; I felt time stop.

'I am getting old, I know. But the feeling came with a vision. As if the universe was being reborn around me, and Miri was the reason for the rebirth. I prefer rebirth, not reboot!' The surgeon chuckled again. 'I thought the vision had lasted a while, that I was having a fit, a seizure, but when it ended, when I came to, I was still feeling her pulse and you were still holding her and I watched the bottle fall from your hand.

'Too many things have happened today. And I have found each one of them hard to accept, or believe, and yet I know they are real. Miri is here, she is real. And I am eighty-two; I cannot believe I have almost completed the Camino. My Camino is real too.' The surgeon was moved and managed to compose himself, he was a professional. 'You are in Monte do Gozo? Yes? Ring from Santiago tomorrow, pray at the cathedral for her full recovery. If she is awake, and we have no more tests, we will arrange for you to see Miri.' The doctor paused, remembering his augur. 'Miri is a miracle. The hospital specialists are referencing my research articles on Miri's condition and saying I have saved her life a second time.' The surgeon gave a nervous laugh. 'I am still trying to understand how I came to the Camino, and be there, in the tunnel, at that precise moment.'

'Thank you, thank you, thank you,' the room shouted before the surgeon ended the call.

'I remember the surgeon from the Camino. I saw him a few times. He was always walking alone,' Sara remembered.

'I remember him too,' Aurora recalled. 'I remember saying *buen Camino*, but I never spoke with him. He always seemed lost in his thoughts.'

Raphael recalled being rescued by the elderly pilgrim on the way down the steep path after the Mountain of Forgiveness.

'Strange,' Keitaro admitted. 'He was in the albergue in Burgos, in the bed next to me. I only said hello. I wonder what stories he would have shared.'

In the morning, waking and putting on their mochilas also woke some unfinished emotions.

'It's like, I do not want to take another step without her near me,' Raphael confessed.

Carmen laughed. 'You have discovered the world of love,' she teased, looking at Keitaro.

The walk to Santiago was tinged with some melancholy. But the entry into the old town was full of smiles and laughs, and entering the hum of Praza Obredorio brought a rush of joy.

'The Pilgrim's mass,' Carmen called. 'It will begin

soon. I want to pray for Miri.'

Just managing to enter before the security team closed the doors, there was standing room only. Raphael perched on a pillar remembering his Camino, Miri, Ava and the surgeon. He looked at all the love around him, flowing through the cathedral. When the voice of a singing nun began, tears also began. Happy tears, grateful tears, painful tears, tears for the future and the past. Tears for Miri to make a full recovery. And Raphael also remembered his ancestors. The generations of flower collectors before him.

Finally, in Rúa do Vilar, with their mochilas gathered around a vacant table in the street, the friends ordered café con leche, *zumo de naranja* and croissant. Smiles, calm, joy and then laughter when the breakfast arrived.

Raphael looked at his phone and pressed redial. The phone was answered immediately.

'We are in Santiago,' Raphael began. 'I hope you have both had a good night's rest. What is the news?'

Raphael listened. And then, without a word, and with a huge grin, he put the phone down.

Everyone waited anxiously.

'She is crazy. So is that surgeon! This morning, Miri woke early and insisted on leaving the hospital. He said they could not keep her in the hospital because her readings and scans showed her to be in almost perfect health. You will not believe…' Raphael paused to catch his breath. 'Miri and the surgeon have already returned to the tunnel where she fell, and are continuing their Camino. They are walking together, now.'

Sara screamed. None could hold their joy. Passers-by in the street asked what was going on.

'What else, what else?' A teary-eyed Carmen wanted more.

'They plan to be in Monte do Gozo tonight.'

'Bus number 17 or shall we walk back?' Keitaro offered instantly, remembering the bus from the previous year.

'Five km? Walk,' Raphael quipped.

49

Consequence

When the seven voices sang in one euphony, 'You have lived. You are better than us,' Miri understood the moment had arrived. A moment for her to return to a new existence. For her body to surrender her living form and for her energy to enter a new realm, a new existence that some called "heaven", others, the afterlife, and yet others knew it to be the enlightenment.

You have loved, been loved. You know beauty and joy. You know what a beginning is. You have experienced life, and you have experienced the end of life. Life is a mystery for us. You are better than us.

Miri was surprised. She found the song of the voices comforting. But with the final resonance of the last sound of the song, Miri became overwhelmed with an uncertainty.

Love is an uncertainty.

Surrendering to love is uncertainty.

Love was more than a word. Unfinished love. Miri had more to learn. More love to offer, more to accept and more love to learn.

If Miri had doubted her purpose before, Miri now understood that her time, her life, had been an existence to allow her to love, be loved, and to love again, to feel love.

And even as her hearts slowed, and even before Miri's body had embraced the song, the seven voices rose to sing for Miri again.

And when you are ready, when you have surrendered to love, you will return to us.

Miri understood that her journey in time, in life, in love was not yet complete.

As threads of the universe began to unravel around her, Miri breathed the consequence of the songs. Whatever was about to happen, she knew her soul was not yet ready to leave her body, that the existence that gave her a journey, called life, was not yet ready for her soul, her energy, to return.

Miri's soul and Miri's body sensed a consummation of a pink force, a pink energy. The pink elixir from a rare flower that grew on the grave of an angel. Miri gripped the pink thread of life that reached her. A thread that sewed her being together, guided her spirit, her soul, back towards a heart that had been silent, and now began beating.

But before the moment could complete itself, Miri was caught by a reverberation. An echo from another world appeared and reached out to meet her. Miri looked towards the unexpected moment. There appeared a face. An irresistible face.

'I know you,' said Miri.

'I am a part of you,' replied the face of the angel,

without a pause. Miri's voice was speaking, but Miri did not recognise her own voice.

'You collected me once, with your hand, and I have since lived a life and loved with you. But now, the song has reached me, and so I must leave you. I must return to my existence. An existence that does not know love, does not know time.'

'That cannot be,' said Miri after a pause. Miri was surprised there was time for a pause. 'You have been part of me. You have been in my hand since I was born. You have experienced the sensations of love with me, you experienced my beginning and my end, you have felt what it is to love and be loved. You were not supposed to part of me. If you take these sensations with you, the universe will know love, the universe will know life.'

The angel paused. 'I will be the first.'

When Miri's fifth heart, her silent heart, woke inside her body, Miri's body connected to her spirit, her soul and returned to her the pink thread of life. The paramedics did not understand.

'She had a chaos of heartbeats a moment ago; it was a heart attack.'

'She had four heart beats before,' the surgeon explained. 'Each heart was shutting down. One by one. Now only one heart is beating. Let us make sure her heartbeat settles.'

He was satisfied that the heartbeat was strong and keeping her alive.

'I remember her hearts,' the surgeon continued. 'Her name is Miri, she was my last patient,' the old man added, introducing himself and laughed. 'It has taken twenty-five years for her hearts to heal.' He laughed again.

The paramedics, the hospital, the nurses and the doctors were confused.

The universe was not confused.

In the universe there are no unknowns. For unknowns always become known. And all knowns have a consequence.

Hari was a spirit. Unlike other spirits, he lived in two moments. Two moments that stretched across all moments in the universe.

By refusing the taking of an oath to protect humans on the mountain of oaths, Hari felt a new awareness of his existence around him.

Consciousness.

Hari had always been at one with the universe. But now he was separate. He was alone.

Having never felt alone before, he wondered about the new emptiness that surrounded him.

Hari felt lost.

And the universe is vast to be lost in.

In the moment of time, Hari looked at the spirit Miri, a spirit about to be born. He saw the energy of the spirit connecting to a physical body. The creation of a soul embodied inside a mother's love. Hari looked with more intrigue at the half-born spirit, and then something most unexpected happened. The half-born Miri reacted the only way her body was designed to in such a moment of confusion, surprise and desire: her sixth sense reached out with one of her tiny hands and grasped tightly the look upon Hari's face. It was spontaneous, unplanned, and, most certainly, unintended. Miri was not supposed to do anything other than be born. Most certainly, she was not supposed to grab hold of the look of an angel.

For Hari, to whom the face belonged, the entire moment was nothing less than a fraction of space.

Sprits were not supposed to know life, love, or time. The consequence for Hari and the universe remained to be discovered.

50

Compostela

The queue for a bed at the albergue in Monte do Gozo was not as subdued or as silent as the day before. Various colourful rumours about a pilgrim's collapse along the Camino and her recovery abounded.

'Did you hear about the miracle on the Camino yesterday? A woman died and came back to life. A Camino miracle!' was the most outrageous rumour circulating.

'Next they will declare Miri a saint!' Raphael joked with Sara.

'A secret, magic potion saved her life,' one insisted. 'I am trying to find out who made it. Apparently an old woman, a recluse, she lives along the Camino. I will find out where she lives.'

Raphael worried for his grandmother and imagined a line of pilgrims at her door, and he laughed at the thought.

And there were a few stranger comments.

'I met one pilgrim who says he saw an angel standing over her, where she fell.'

Another offered, 'My friend was there. He saw what happened. He described a large man running away after the pilgrim fell. He tried to steal her money. He was wearing a large San Fermín hat with bull horns to hide his face. The police asked him to make a witness statement and apparently the police are looking for the man he described.'

Miri and the surgeon were calmly cooking in a packed kitchen.

'Pasta with tuna?' Miri offered casually. And then came the screams and the well-earned hugs, the longest from Raphael.

It was the turn of the surgeon to weep when each pilgrim hugged him one by one. A hug of gratitude, and none could hold the tears when they watched Miri hug the surgeon.

That night, Miri listened to her heart.

'Can anyone hear the rhythm of the world?' Miri asked from her bed.

'The music is different now,' the surgeon replied. 'Does not sound like the Beatles any more.'

'How old are you?' Keitaro had to ask.

There were many laughs in the albergue. But no reply.

The next morning, when they entered the old town of Santiago, Miri insisted they hold each other's hands in a line as they walked through the town to the cathedral. The streets were wide enough and many locals, being used to pilgrims, welcomed the sight and moved aside to let them pass.

The surgeon was very moved by the act. He had

started the Camino alone and finished with Miri and a new Camino family. And when they reached the stone shell of the Compostela, in the middle of the Praza, they formed a circle around the plaque, still holding hands. The sight of the surgeon's joy and streams of tears on each other's faces drew them all to Camino memories and hugs and more shared tears.

'This was my last dream. A promise I had made to your mother, Miri. Seems the promise brought me back to you.'

Miri threw her rucksack to the floor and lay on the floor. They all jumped down with Miri for a group photo in front of the cathedral.

And the sunbeams reached through the cathedral spires to bless the group.

Raphael collected that moment. It would be one of the most precious moments in his collection. One day, many lives later, he would be the collector of moments and open his entire collection to the world of angels and spirits.

It was Sara who used the dreaded words first.

'I have to leave, I have to get to the bus stop.'

There, in front of the cathedral, they stood again, and screamed and shouted their joy and hugged once more and wept their farewell.

The silent family, a mother, a father and a teenage daughter, having just arrived at the stone of the Compostela, turned towards the shouting.

'What is that, dear?' asked the father with slight

alarm.

Mother was already staring.

'Love,' she said, without hesitation.

The teenage voice, next to the mother, also replied, 'I would like some of that.'